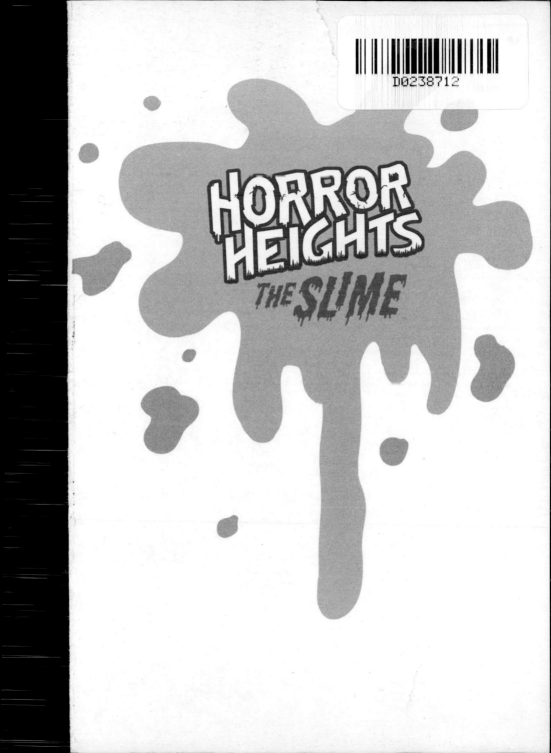

HORROR HEIGHTS

THE SLIME

BEC HILL

HORROR HEIGHTS

THE SLIME

ILLUSTRATIONS
by BERAT
PEKMEZCI

HODDER

HODDER CHILDREN'S BOOKS

First published in Great Britain in 2021 by Hodder & Stoughton

1 3 5 7 9 10 8 6 4 2 1

A CIP catalogue record for this book is available from the
British Library.

ISBN 978 1 444 96229 1

Typeset in Sassoon Infant by Avon DataSet Ltd, Arden Road,
Alcester, Warwickshire

Printed and bound in Great Britain by Clays Ltd, Elcograf S.p.A.

The paper and board used in this book
are made from wood from responsible sources.

Hodder Children's Books
An imprint of
Hachette Children's Group
Part of Hodder & Stoughton Limited
Carmelite House
50 Victoria Embankment
London EC4Y 0DZ

An Hachette UK Company
www.hachette.co.uk

www.hachettechildrens.co.uk

A NOTE FROM THE AUTHOR

In my travels around the world as a writer, comedian and TV presenter, I've heard my fair share of spooky stories and strange happenings. Every town, neighbourhood, or community has one. But one place in particular stood out from the rest. It didn't have one unexplained event – it had THIRTEEN. Weirder still, they all occurred between the SAME dates *and* to individuals at the SAME school. I have been fortunate enough to be granted access to classified reports and exclusive interviews with the people involved so that their experiences can be anonymously shared without affecting any current investigations.

For the purposes of privacy and safety, names have been changed and I have dubbed the location "Horror Heights". If any of the incidents mentioned within these books have happened to you, or if you believe you might live in "Horror Heights", please report it to an adult you trust. Stay safe and remember: *follow the recipe* ...

Bec Hill

FRIDAY

CHAPTER 1

"NOOOOOOooooooooo!!!" cried Connie.

But it was too late. Ms Strapp was heading to the Confiscation Cupboard in the staffroom with Connie's latest tub of slime. Again.

"Why does she ALWAYS do that?" Connie sulked.

"Maybe it would be better if you didn't bring your slime collection to school?" suggested Allyce, in a kind tone.

Connie's second-best friend was always trying to work out a better way to do things. A faster way to run. A quicker way to do homework. Allyce had even worked out the most efficient way to disarm someone in a fight (throw something in their face).

"I can't leave the tubs at home!" said Connie. "Then no one will know that I'm Connie Queen of Slime!"

"Actually," said JD, leaning back in their chair. "If Ms Strapp has them all, then that makes HER the Queen of Slime ..."

"Quit being a sasspot, JD!" said Amy. She turned to Connie. "You nearly made a whole week without getting it confiscated! Better luck next time."

Amy was superstitious (and Connie's *other* second-best friend). Some kids thought she was a bit bonkers, but that's what made her so much fun to be around.

Allyce and Amy kept chatting, shouting over Connie, whose desk was between them. She liked the fact that her desk was sandwiched between her friends, but hearing them in stereo could be a bit overwhelming sometimes.

"What do you think Ms Strapp does with all the slime?" asked Allyce.

"I think she EATS them!" Amy replied.

"I think she takes them home and pours them

all into her bath and then just lies in it!" said Allyce, bursting into giggles.

"Yeah!" said Amy, struggling to contain her laughter. "In the NUDE!"

Connie clasped her hands over her ears. The thought of her slime being anywhere near her teacher's exposed buttocks was enough to make her woozy.

Something tickled the back of her neck. She quickly slapped it, in case it was a spider and Ryan was filming one of his dumb pranks on his phone again. Thankfully, it was just a note from Nat, who sat behind her.

Cheer up!
It's nearly the weekend!

DaVerse tonight?

Connie grinned. DaVerse (short for Danger Universe) was an online game where players could team up to complete tasks (like slay a dragon, or escape a dungeon, or open a hat shop). Her first-best friend, Nat, was her questing partner. The pair were almost opposites: Nat was calm, rational and precise, while Connie was restless, silly and spontaneous. But when they worked together, they were invincible.

She turned around and gave Nat a double thumbs-up, just as Ms Strapp marched back in.

Ms Strapp wasn't a tall lady, but she walked like she was. She always looked pensive, as if she was trying to do a crossword in her head and couldn't work out the final clue. No one had ever seen her smile. Legend said she once came close, but the only kid who was there at the time passed out in terror before they saw her lips form a complete grin.

As Ms Strapp made her way to the front of the class, everyone sat up straight again, except for

Amy, who was still giggling at the image of Ms Strapp bathing in slime. Her shoulders shook. Allyce whispered out the corner of her mouth in Amy's direction.

"Slimy Strapp ..."

Amy's shoulders vibrated. A single tear rolled down her cheek as she attempted to stifle the sniggers escaping her mouth. Allyce continued.

"... and her blobby bum bum ..."

Amy exploded with a loud snort laugh, shocking everyone – including Ms Strapp.

"What seems to be so funny, Amy?" their teacher asked sternly.

Amy composed herself. "Ah, just, uh. A funny meme I remembered."

"Fascinating. You can draw it for me *after* class."

"But I've got rehearsals for the Horror Heights play!"

"Well, I guess you're going to be late, aren't you?"

Amy knew better than to argue any further. "I might as well be cursed," she muttered under her breath.

As if giving a kid detention for giggling wasn't bad enough, Ms Strapp then gave everyone homework. They had to make a poster about ancient Egypt over the weekend.

Connie hated poster projects. They either had to be really well-researched or really artistic, and Connie wasn't good at research OR art.

The bell rang and Ms Strapp dismissed the class. Allyce apologised to Amy and offered to wait around for her to finish detention.

"I'd wait too," added Connie. "But I don't want Dad to go shopping without me. I need a new slime!"

"What happened to that one your aunty sent you?" asked Nat.

"It shrivelled up into a little piece of plastic, remember?" said Connie. "Dust. Slime's worst enemy!"

"You're so lucky your dad buys you slime," said Amy.

Nat raised an eyebrow at Connie. She was the only one who knew the truth about how Connie got her slime. But, like a true first-best friend, she didn't say anything.

"Yeah," added Allyce. "My mum never buys me new stuff."

"Isn't she getting you a phone for your birthday in a few weeks?" Connie reminded her, with a tinge of envy.

"Yeah," Allyce said. "But I've promised to only use it for phone calls and training. I'm gonna link my fitness tracker to it, so I can trace my running routes."

"If I had a phone, I'd watch slime videos,

like, all the time," said Connie.

"That's why you're not allowed one," said Nat. She grinned, without looking up. She was the only one in their group who had a phone and she was already using it to research facts for her weekend assignment.

Connie looked over Nat's shoulder. "Does it say anything about whether the ancient Egyptians were allowed phones?"

"Well, they did have tablets," said Nat, with a wink.

Connie groan-laughed and picked up her bag.

"Remember," she whispered to Amy, as she left. "If Ms Strapp smiles, don't look directly at it."

CHAPTER 2

Connie walked quickly, as if her life depended on it. In some ways, it did.

If her dad got home before her, it meant he went shopping without her. Which meant she couldn't get a new slime. Which meant she could lose her reputation as "Connie Queen of Slime".

She was given her title earlier that year. Everyone in her class was told to bring in an item related to their hobby – and she had nothing to bring in.

In fact, she didn't have a hobby (unless you counted watching TV or gaming, and Ms Strapp had made it *very* clear that she didn't). She was the only kid in the final year of primary school without an obvious skill. Even her friends had special talents: Nat was nerdy, Amy was artistic, and Allyce was athletic. Compared to those around her, Connie felt very ordinary.

However, the day before they had to present their items, she randomly received a Bouncy Roo Poo Slime in the post from her aunty. Connie had never shown an interest in slime — and she had certainly never asked for it — but without anything else to talk about, she took it to school.

Her improvised presentation about being a "slime collector" was a surprising success. Her classmates found her made-up hobby so amusing, they dubbed her "Connie Queen of Slime" and she no longer felt ordinary: she felt *extraordinary*.

To keep her title, Connie became an *actual* slime collector. It wasn't easy — her allowance was pitiful and her dad wouldn't buy it — so she had been forced to develop ...

THE 4-STEP SLIME HEIST PLAN

STEP 1: The Helpful Assistant

Connie would help her dad do the grocery shopping and make sure he didn't miss ANYTHING on his list. The more items at the checkout, the better ...

STEP 2: The Sprint

While Connie's dad was busy squeezing every avocado to see which ones were ripe, Connie would run to "the forbidden aisle" (the one with all the toys and party supplies that her dad refused to go down). She would pick a new slime and hide it in her hand. (FUN FACT: Magicians call this "palming".)

STEP 3: The Misdirect

At the checkout, Connie would point to the latest *Clash of the Cakes with Helen Melon* magazine. She'd say something like, "Look, Dad! Top tips for a good, gooey pud!" It ALWAYS worked. Baking was his weakness. While he was distracted, she could implement ...

STEP 4: The Switch

Connie would add the slime she palmed earlier to the conveyor belt for the server to scan, then swiftly pocket it again before her dad saw. He would pay for all the shopping, totally unaware that he was also buying Connie's latest slime.

Connie's slime heists meant that she always had a new slime to bring in and show off. Glittery unicorn slime, smelly sewer slime, glow-in-the-dark radioactive slime: you name it, Connie had heisted it (and Ms Strapp had confiscated it). She felt bad about tricking her dad, but she was fully committed to her new identity and didn't plan on losing it.

Then again, she also didn't plan on what would happen after she got home that day ...

CHAPTER 3

Connie's flat wasn't huge, but it had everything she and her dad needed. The entrance opened into the living room with a small kitchen closed off to the left. On the opposite side of the living room was the hallway which had Connie's room on the right and the main bathroom to the left. At the far end of the hall was her dad's room. He had his own en suite bathroom, so Connie couldn't hear his singing in the shower, or his bowel movements on the loo. She was eternally grateful for that.

When she got home from school, she opened the door and threw her school bag at the little round dining table just ahead of her. It missed by a mile and slammed into the wall.

"Oi!" came an unexpected voice. "Is this what you do when I'm not home?"

It gave Connie a fright. She peered left around

the corner into the rest of the living room.

Her dad was lying on the couch with his foot bandaged up. It turned out that he'd hurt it at work and a doctor had sent him home to rest. It wasn't serious, but it looked swollen, so she went to fetch some frozen peas for it.

When she opened the kitchen door, she was hit by an unsettling stench.

"Oof, Dad! Did you fart?" Connie asked. She pinched her nose. "Gross! It smells like dirty socks in here!"

"Is it the bins? I hope not! It's not Bin Day until Monday!"

Connie checked both the rubbish and recycling bins in the corner of the kitchen near the door. They smelled fine.

Her dad appeared, hopping on one leg. "Pooey!" He waved a hand in front of his nose. "Connie! You stinker!"

"It wasn't me!!!" she insisted.

"I'm joking!" said her dad, with a laugh. "It's my Mother!"

Connie screwed her face up, confused. "Gran's here?"

"No!" Her dad pointed to a jar resting on the counter, as if that somehow explained everything. "The Mother! It's a mix of yeast and bacteria, so I can bake my own sourdough bread!"

"Ew, Dad! That's rank."

"Aww, don't say that in front of the Mother! You know it's a living organism, right?" He held the jar, pretending to cover its ears.

Connie stuck her tongue out. Her dad went to ruffle her hair, but lost his balance and stood on his bad foot.

"Ow!"

Connie helped him back to the sofa. Her dad

could be annoying sometimes (and embarrassing), but she didn't want him to be in pain. Anyway, she needed him to get better quickly, so they could go to the shops for more stealth slime!

"Thanks, Con," her dad said, settling back on the cushions. "You're a good kid. The best! It's so nice of you to let me rest …"

"No problem," said Connie.

"*And* to make me a cup of tea …" he said, flashing a cheeky grin.

"Fine." Connie rolled her eyes and headed back to the kitchen to pop the kettle on, holding her nose to fend off the stench.

CHAPTER 4

It was getting dangerously near the supermarket closing time and Connie's dad was STILL lying on the sofa with his tablet. She stood in front of him, dancing from foot to foot.

"Con, do you need a wee? Have you forgotten how to use a big person toilet? Shall I lay out some newspaper?" he joked.

"Daaaa-aaaad! It's getting late! We have to go do the weekly shop!"

"Oh, that? I've already done it!" he said proudly, waving his tablet. "I ordered the groceries on my MASSIVE PHONE!" (Ages ago, he had called his tablet a "massive phone" for a joke. Connie made the mistake of laughing so he started doing it all. The. Time.) "It should be delivered Monday night! How cool is that?"

WHAT?! The colour drained from her face. She couldn't be the Queen of Slime if she didn't have any slime!

Connie ran to her room and frantically searched amongst the mess. She figured she MUST have a spare slime SOMEWHERE!

She checked under the bed: nothing. She checked in her school bag: nothing. She even checked the bottom drawer, which she never used. It had fidget spinners, food-themed erasers, loom bands and – *AH HAH!* – a slime tub!

She peeled back the lid – *Noooo!* – it was her old, dusty, dried up Bouncy Roo Poo Slime! She couldn't take THAT to school!

"Wow, I guess I missed the warning about Hurricane Connie!" said her dad, leaning against her bedroom doorway, like a pirate on one leg. He surveyed the mess. "What's got into you?"

"I – I need some slime for school on Monday," she explained. It wasn't exactly a lie.

"What, like for a science experiment?"

"Uh … YEAH!" she said.

"Hmm … Why don't you make some?"

Connie's heart sank. He didn't get it. Everyone could tell home-made slime from REAL slime. It stained your hands, smelled like glue and was always *too* slimy.

"No, I need the proper stuff," said Connie.

"Nonsense!" her dad insisted. "I bet you'll get bonus marks for making it yourself! And all your friends will think you're really smart and cool. I'll find a slime recipe on my MASSIVE PHONE!"

He hobbled off and Connie sighed. Could things get ANY worse?

Yes.

Yes they could.

CHAPTER 5

The enormous dragon towered over Connie and Nat, ready to devour them both. They'd been trying to complete their quest for weeks. All they had to do was destroy the final boss, but it was impervious to their attacks. A message from Nat popped up in the DaVerse chatbox:

Nat831415
I think we have to be more logical. What's a fire-breathing dragon's biggest weakness?

Connie looked around the dungeon they were fighting in and spotted something on the floor.

conluvspizzacake
got it

She dived, grabbing the fire extinguisher. She took aim and released a spray of foam into the dragon's jaws. The dragon gulped, blinked and then

EXPLODED, showering their two avatars in gold coins and guts.

Nat831415
THAT WAS AMAZING!

conluvspizzacake
couldnt have done it without you

Connie's stomach gurgled.

conluvspizzacake
g2g eat byyyeeeeeee

She shut her dad's laptop and took it back to the living room.

"Daaaaaad, what's for dinner?"

"Pizza Cake!" he announced, looking up from his tablet. "I thought you might need the kitchen to make your slime, so I ordered in. You should have time before it arrives." He held up a piece of paper for her to take.

It was a slime recipe he had copied from a website with a little cartoon blob drawn in the corner. Connie felt a pang of guilt about her slime heists.

She decided it was worth giving it a shot. Most kids failed when they tried to make slime, but what if it was Connie's hidden talent? What if she could make it just as good as the stuff in the shops, or even better? What if it was so good that she could sell it and pay her dad back for all the tubs of slime he had unknowingly bought?

As she entered the kitchen, the smell of the Mother slapped her across the face like a damp pair of pants. Connie held her breath, rolled up her sleeves and got to work.

After what felt like HOURS of measuring and mixing (but was only about ten minutes), Connie finally had her slime. Except it smelled like glue, stained her hands green and was TOO slimy. It definitely wasn't her hidden talent.

"Yikes," she said.

Connie wasn't ready to give up quite so easily, though. She enjoyed thinking on her feet and hoped she could fix it with some extra ingredients.

First, she needed something which made stuff less wet. She remembered the foot powder her dad bought in bulk from the street market. He used it to dry out his sweaty shoes after basketball, but he kept it in his en suite because the label said children shouldn't use it.

Fortunately, he had nodded off on the couch, so Connie quietly ran to his room and grabbed the massive tub from his bathroom. She scooped a few spoonfuls into the bowl and watched as the mixture started to thicken up.

It was working well. A little TOO well. It became less like slime and more like ... cement. She tried to knead it with her green-stained hands, but the dense concoction turned them bright blue.

She pumped some liquid soap into her palms to wash it off.

OF COURSE! she thought. Soap!

If liquid soap could wash the colour off her hands, then it could probably prevent her slime from staining them in the first place. It could even make the mix slimy again.

Connie emptied the bottle of liquid soap into the bowl and stirred it all together. The mixture stopped staining her hands and became the perfect consistency. But it still smelled like glue.

If slime smelled like glue, it was a dead giveaway that it was home-made. Each slime from the shops had a special scent, like yummy cotton candy or revolting rotten eggs. Connie's slime needed a unique aroma. It needed to be bold. Brave. Daring! She took a deep breath and it hit her:

DIRTY SOCKS!

Connie picked up her dad's jar of Mother and carefully unscrewed the lid. The stink was even worse than before. She heard a snort from the living room and froze. If her dad caught her messing with the Mother, she'd be in deep trouble!

She peeped into the living room. Her dad was still dozing. He rolled over, twitching his nose.

"Ooh, excuse ME, Ambassador. I seem to have passed wind," he murmured.

She was safe. She reversed back into the kitchen and held her breath, partly due to nerves and partly because it stank.

One teaspoon of the Mother was all it took. The slime smelled EXACTLY like dirty socks.

Before Connie could celebrate, the slime turned yellowy-brown, like a cross between mustard and poo.

Okay … Connie thought.

Then the slime began to bubble.

Oh my!

THEN the slime became hot. REALLY hot.

Oh no!

Connie felt nervous. She recalled a science lesson where Ms Strapp told them that being irresponsible with chemicals could lead to painful burns. She quickly spooned the heaving mixture into the rubbish bin, being careful not to touch it.

"Big yikes!" she muttered. "So much for Connie Queen of Slime!"

CHAPTER 6

"At least you tried, kiddo," said Connie's dad through a mouthful of pizza.

She hadn't told him about the extra ingredients she'd added to the slime recipe.

"Don't think I've forgotten about the state of your room, though," he added, tossing the last crust back into the box. "I don't want mice again. You'd better clean it tomorrow. In fact, you can get some practice in now!" He passed her the pizza box. "Remember — rubbish goes in the bin with the blue lid and recycling goes in the bin with the ..."

"Yellow lid. Yeah, yeah," Connie sighed and headed to the kitchen. It smelled worse than before thanks to her failed slime experiment sitting in the bin.

"Hey, it's YOUR planet, Con! You gotta look after it!"

Truth was, she DID care about the planet and was usually very careful when it came to recycling. But the pizza box was the perfect size to cover up the slime and stop the smell from escaping, so she wedged it into the bin with the blue lid and got ready for bed.

That night Connie dreamt she was a REAL Queen and she owned ALL the slime in the WORLD! She had maids who cleaned her room and did her homework for her. Ms Strapp apologised for being so mean all the time. And everyone cheered her name as she walked through the school.

Connie Queen of Slime! Connie Queen of Slime!

SATURDAY

CHAPTER 7

"CONNIE QUEEN OF SLIME!"

Connie woke up with a start. She could swear someone had yelled out her name. The sun was up, but only just. Her room was still a mess from the day before and it smelled like ... *dirty socks*?

She rolled over to check the time, only to be confronted by a pair of unblinking eyes.

There, on her pillow, the size of a sandwich, was a disgusting, yellowy-brown blob. It beamed a gummy grin.

"CONNIE QUEEN OF SLIME!" it yelled.

Connie yelped as she jumped out of bed and flung her pillow away from her. The slime went flying across the room and into the wall with a SPLAT.

"Wheeeee!" the slime said in a muffled voice, as it slid squishily to the floor.

Connie felt bad about flinging it so hard. She climbed back on to the bed. "Little blob?" she called in a quiet, scared voice. "Are you okay?"

She peered over the edge of the bed, trying to distinguish what was floor, what was mess and what could be blob ...

"CONNIE QUEEN OF SLIME!" yelled the blob from behind her.

Connie yelped again and toppled off the end of the bed, bumping her head on the ground. "Ow!"

"Oh no!" squealed the slime, looking down at her from the edge of the bed. Something that vaguely resembled an arm stretched out and softly patted her head. "Pat, pat," it said.

Connie was too scared to move.

"What ... no, WHO ... are ... you?" she managed to stutter.

"Big!" exclaimed the slime as it retracted its arm back into itself.

"Big?"

"Yes!" confirmed the slime cheerily. "Connie Queen of Slime, call me Big Yikes!"

Big Yikes? It sounded familiar …

"Oh my gosh! YOU'RE the slime I made yesterday?"

"Yes! Connie Queen of Slime make Big Yikes! Then give Big Yikes nice warm house! Then give Big Yikes tasty hards!"

"Nice warm house?"

"Like dis!" said Big, pointing to her bin.

"Ah! I see … And what are tasty hards?"

"Mmm!!!! Tasty hards!" repeated Big, rubbing its belly with its little blobby arms.

Connie tried to remember what she'd thrown

into the bin the night before.

"Do you mean the pizza crusts?"

"Mmm! Yes! More tasty hards for Big?" it asked, giving Connie puppy dog eyes. It looked almost ... cute. Like a baby ... made of jelly ... a jelly baby. But bigger. Like a jelly baby who'd eaten all the other jelly babies.

Connie couldn't believe it. Either she was the victim of a very elaborate prank, or she was ACTUALLY having a conversation with a living slime. A slime SHE'D made. If it was real, then she was going to be rich! Every kid in school would want one!

At that moment, Connie heard a thumping sound. It started faint and then grew louder and louder. It was her dad, hopping towards her room. As nice as he was, he was a bit jumpy when it came to animals and *very* allergic. She once saw him freak out and flatten a mouse with a frying pan. It was eating a piece of cheese on her bedroom floor which she'd secretly left out for it. She had always felt guilty about that.

"Daddy!" squealed Big, as it oozed towards her door. "Daddy have tasty hards?"

Connie panicked. "No! Daddy have no tasty har— Why am I talking like you? Dad won't have any pizza crusts. You have to stay quiet."

Just then, a loud scream came from the other side of her bedroom door, causing her to jump. Big slid behind her, trembling.

"Dad? You okay?" she called.

"Yeah! I'm just – AHHH-CHAAAHHHH!!!! – sneezing!" he called back.

Ah. Her dad was having a screezing fit.

"Screeze" was a word coined by Connie to describe her dad's scream-sneezes. They were so sudden and forceful that, even though Connie knew he wasn't in danger, they always gave her a fright.

Her dad gave a gentle knock before popping his head into her room. "Morning Con," he began, but then he noticed the room and started spluttering. "WHOA! It STINKS in here! And no wonder — this room is a tip! You really need to tidy it. Look at all this stuff!"

He picked up a cap from the floor. As he lifted it towards his head, Connie noticed Big hiding inside it, grasping on to the edges of the rim.

"NO!" Connie yelled, leaping up and snatching the hat from her dad

"Wow, do you really think it will look *that* bad on me? Charming!"

"No! It's just ... I wanted to wear it!" Connie said, quickly putting it on.

She felt the warm stickiness of the slime as it hugged the top of her head. The smell was overpowering. She winced, but managed to smile as if everything was fine.

"Okay, you big weirdo!" her dad said, turning to leave.

"Not Big Weirdo! Big Yikes!" came a muffled reply from her hat.

Connie's dad turned back around. "Did you say something?"

"Uhh ..." She looked around her room. "Big yikes! Look how messy this room is! I'd better clean it up!"

"Atta girl! If you get all your chores done this weekend, I'll order pizza again tomorrow night!"

"Tasty hards!" Big burbled into Connie's hair.

"What's that, Con?"

"Tasty! ... Hard ... work ... will pay off!" She smiled awkwardly and then gave him a thumbs-up.

He gave a thumbs-up back and hopped off.

When she was certain the coast was clear, Connie pulled off her cap, but Big wasn't inside it.

"Big? Big!" she whispered.

"Connie Queen of Slime?" Big whispered back. The slime was still hugging her head.

Connie plucked the clingy creature off and plonked it on to her bedside table. She grabbed some clothes from a pile on the floor and headed for the bathroom. She figured a quick shower would help her gather her thoughts and get rid of the stink radiating from her hair.

"I'll be back soon. You stay here, okay?" she said. If Big was real (and not a figment of her imagination), she couldn't risk it roaming around the house, looking for pizza crusts and scaring her dad.

"Okay," said Big. "Anything for Connie Queen of Slime."

CHAPTER 8

In the shower, Connie reflected on the recent turn of events and decided her mind was playing tricks on her. Nat had once told her about a condition where your body wakes up in the morning, but your brain thinks it's still asleep and carries on dreaming. Once she felt more refreshed, she knew Big Yikes had just been a weird hallucination.

She got dressed and held her breath as she opened her bedroom door. There was nothing there.

Relief washed over her with a hint of disappointment. Nothing except her boring, messy room.

And the pungent stench of dirty socks.

Is it possible to hallucinate smells? she thought.

Sniffing the air, Connie got down on all

fours, like a dog sussing out the perfect pee spot in the park. The smell was coming from her backpack — her lunchbox to be exact. She peeled back the lid ...

"YAY!" cheered the slime. "You find Big! Connie hide now!"

It was no hallucination. Connie had somehow managed to create a sentient slime creature with the ability to play hide-and-seek.

She wondered what else it could do ...

CHAPTER 9

Connie spent all morning teaching Big Yikes various tricks and games in her room. By lunch, the slime could fetch, roll over, beg and high-five. It was also surprisingly good at DaVerse, considering it was only a day old and didn't have any thumbs.

Big was so keen to learn and help that Connie began to feel quite proud of her phlegm-like little friend. She couldn't wait to take it to school on Monday and show it off to her classmates. The Bouncy Roo Poo Slime was *nothing* compared to Big Yikes!

Their playing was interrupted by more of her dad's screezes coming from the living room.

"AAAAHHH-CHAAAHHH!! Have you cleaned your room yet? Either we have mice, or – AAAAHHHHH-CHAAAHHH!! – an abundance of – AAAHHHH-CHAHHH!!! – dust!" he yelled.

Connie knew the truth. It wasn't mice or dust. Her dad was allergic to the secret intelligent blob she was harbouring in her room. She realised she could never tell him about Big. At best, her dad would be impressed, but make her get rid of it because of his allergy. At worst, he would freak out like he did with the mouse and fetch the frying pan ...

The screezing continued. Connie was going to have to get Big out of the flat for a while before her dad got suspicious.

But where?

She couldn't take Big to see her friends yet because they were all busy on Saturdays: Nat tutored her cousins, Amy had rehearsals for her play, and Allyce was training for the 100m sprint in the Community Sports Tournament. Plus, she didn't know if Big was ready to meet other people just yet. She didn't want her little slime to feel scared or upset. What Connie needed was somewhere where Big could observe people at a distance. Somewhere safe.

Somewhere, she thought, catching a whiff of Big's distinctive odour, *with plenty of fresh air* …

Connie hurried past her dad in the living room. Big was hiding quietly in her backpack, nestled between her lunchbox and water bottle.

"School on a Saturday?" her dad said, blowing his nose.

"I'm going for a walk in the park!" she said. She pointed her thumb at the bag on her back. "Taking water and snacks."

"Good idea. Sorry I can't join you," her dad replied, nodding at his swollen ankle. "The doctor told me not to leave home while I'm on my medication, or I might fall asleep and end up in a hole or something!"

"But what about the game tomorrow?" Connie asked, concerned. Her dad volunteered as the Under 13s basketball coach and they were in the Community Sports Tournament the next day. She had no interest in basketball, but she knew the event meant a lot to him. "Can they compete without you there?"

"They'll have to," he sighed. "But they're very talented. They won't need me."

Connie gave him a comforting hug and kissed him on the head.

"Kiss, kiss," said her backpack in a muffled voice.

Her dad raised an eyebrow.

"Oops," said Connie, blushing "Just did some squeaky farts."

He burst out laughing, which eventually turned into another series of screezes.

"I'll vacuum when I get back – promise!" Connie yelled, heading out the door.

CHAPTER 10

Once Connie was a safe distance from her flat, she swung her backpack on to her front and undid the zip. Big peered out from the opening but made sure to stay hidden as instructed by Connie. She felt like a parent carrying their baby in a harness. The slime's eyes grew wide as it took in the sight of the blue sky, the warmth of the sunshine and the sound of the birds in the trees.

Big's voice floated up through the open zip as they passed something by the pavement, "Park?"

Connie chuckled. "Nope! That's a post box!"

Big continued to ask if other things were parks: bins, streetlights, small children … It was cute at first, but after a while Connie started to feel like an exhausted babysitter.

She took a path between some houses, which

ran through some dense trees and over a small creek before coming out into a clearing.

"THIS is a park!" Connie announced as they reached their destination.

The little blob fell silent (much to Connie's relief). It was in awe. She pointed out the park's playground to the left, the picnic area to the right and, ahead in the distance, the outdoor basketball court the park shared with her school.

Big was keen to see Connie's school, but as she neared the court, she noticed a lone figure was shooting hoops. It was Mike, a kid from her class. They had never hung out together, so Connie didn't know much about him other than the fact that he was on the Under 13s team. She wondered if he had heard about her dad's injury.

I should probably tell him, she thought.

But then she hesitated. Her gut told her to protect Big.

Connie whispered into her bag, "I might need you to stay super quiet for a moment again, okay?"

"More hide-and-seek?" asked the slime.

"Yes, but just the hide part for now."

"Okay, Big hide ... for now."

Big obediently ducked down so Connie could zip the bag up.

"Hey!" she called as she approached the court, giving a little wave.

It caught Mike by surprise, causing him to twitch while shooting and miss the hoop. He spun around and glared.

"What do you want, Kenny??" he demanded.

"Uh, it's Connie ..." she said, too taken aback by his attitude to be offended.

"That's it. Slime girl. Our coach is your dad, right?" he said, fetching the ball.

Connie nodded. "Yeah. Did you hear he hurt himself? He can't make the game tomorrow ..."

Mike snapped. "What, he's giving up on us because he has a little boo boo?!"

Connie was shocked at his lack of empathy and wanted to scream at him for being so rude about her dad. But she didn't want to frighten Big, who was still sitting silently at the bottom of her bag.

She tried to calm Mike down. "He believes in the team. You're all talented enough to win without him there."

"And what would you know about talent?"

Connie's throat went suddenly dry. "Excuse me?"

"I'm just sayin'," Mike said, bouncing the ball. "Everyone in our class seems to have a talent. Shaun bakes. Clarinda dances. I'm a great Point Guard. What's *your* talent, Kenny?"

"I'm Connie …" she whispered, feeling like the air had just been sucked out of her. "Queen of Slime …" she added. But it sounded so pathetic.

Without breaking eye contact, Mike threw the ball backwards over his shoulder. It sailed clean through the hoop. He didn't even look back to check. He just smirked.

"Slime isn't a talent."

Connie opened her mouth to defend herself, but nothing came out. She just stood there. Mike retrieved the ball and took another shot. It flew effortlessly through the hoop.

"Tell your dad he's right. We don't need him. Not when we have my talent and THESE two bad boys!" he said, kissing his arms. "You take care, Kenny."

"IT CONNIE!!!" shouted Big, bursting out of the top of Connie's backpack.

She was still wearing the bag on her front and

the slime had unzipped it from the inside. Connie tried to push the slime back in, but it was unexpectedly strong and forced her hands out of the way. Big stretched higher and higher until it loomed over Mike, submerging the boy in its shadow. Its voice deepened as it grew.

"CONNIE. QUEEN. OF. SLIME."

Mike practically soiled himself.

And as quickly as it appeared, Big shrank back down into the bag and zipped it up.

Mike was speechless.

Connie smiled. "I'll let Dad know. Thanks, MARK."

She strode away, leaving Mike to gather himself.

A whisper came from Connie's bag, "Big do bad at hide-and-seek."

She unzipped the top so she could see her

little slime.

"No, Big do good," she assured. "Big do good."

CHAPTER 11

Connie wanted to take a moment to process what had happened with Mike, but Big was back to asking questions.

"What that?"

"That's a tree."

"What that?"

"That's a bench."

"What that?"

"That's the same tree again."

Connie was starting to attract odd glances from other people. It looked like she was walking around with her backpack on her front, naming things she saw ... to herself. It was time to go home.

As they headed back through the centre of the park, Big began to jiggle up and down excitedly in her bag. "Oooh! What THAT?"

"That's a water fountain," said Connie. She pointed to the bit where the water flowed out at the top. "See the statue? It's a dog with its leg up. The person who made this designed it so that it looks like the dog is weeing …"

Connie trailed off. She had never had to describe the fountain to someone else before, so she had never considered how ridiculous it was. It had been there her whole life, so she thought it was normal. She wondered if there were any other weird things in Horror Heights, which people just assumed were normal.

"Oooh, shinies!" said Big, leaning out of the bag, pointing at the coins people had thrown into the fountain.

"No, stay in the backpack!" exclaimed Connie, but just as the words came out of her mouth, Big lurched out of the bag and fell into the water.

"Hel-pa, Co-nee Quee—" it gurgled with its arms outstretched. The tiny, helpless slime creature splashed about, panicking. It couldn't swim! Its face was full of complete shock and fear.

Quick as a flash, Connie scooped Big out and plopped it into her bag. It coughed and spluttered before looking up at her with doting eyes.

"Connie Queen of Slime save Big!" It looked at the water bottle in Connie's bag and gave a little shiver. "Big no like water."

Connie emptied her bottle on to the pavement.

"It's all right, you're safe. Come on buddy, let's get you home."

CHAPTER 12

It was late afternoon by the time Connie got home from the park. Her dad was attempting to vacuum on one foot, unsuccessfully.

"I told you I'd do that later," Connie tutted. "You're not supposed to be up!"

"I was just trying to be useful," said her dad, giving up and hopping back to the couch. "How was your walk?"

Connie grunted. "I saw Mike."

Her dad perked up. "How is he? Did you tell him about my injury?"

"Yeah! And he was a real jerk about it!"

Connie's dad scrunched his face up. "Really? Mike? Huh …" He stewed it over for a second. "Well, maybe he's just nervous about the gaaAAAHHHHHHH-CHAAAAHHHHHH!!!"

"Bless you!" said Connie, swiftly heading to her room to get Big away from her dad's sensitive nose. "Chat later!"

When she opened the door, she almost didn't notice the dirty-socks smell. She'd grown used to it. When she opened her bag on the bed, the slime was curled up into a teeny ball with its eyes closed.

Oh no! she thought. *Is it ... dead?*

She lightly prodded Big and it slowly opened its eyes.

"Big Yikes tired," it said in a weary voice, before slowly sliding out of Connie's bag, off her bed and into the bin by her desk. It covered itself in a blanket of used tissues and closed its eyes again. "Night, night, Connie Queen of Slime."

It was so unbelievably cute that Connie just had to share it. She grabbed her dad's tablet from the living room and sent Nat a message.

> **Look what I made!!!**

She snapped a photo of Big tucked up in the tissues, fast asleep. She could tell from the tick next to Nat's name that Nat was online. She waited with nervous excitement, knowing how impressed her best friend was going to be ...

> NAT
> **Ew!**

Puzzled, Connie looked at the picture again. With Big's eyes closed, it did look a bit like she'd taken a photo of a giant yellowy-brown snot in a tissue. Or something worse.

> **I'll show you properly before we go to Allyce's race tomorrow.**

> NAT
> **No thanks. Might be better to show a doctor?**

Connie logged out of her account. She knew Nat would understand when she saw Big in person. She switched the light off so Big could sleep in peace and went to vacuum the living room.

When Connie eventually returned later to go to bed, Big was still snoozing happily in her bin.

Poor little slime, she thought. *All tuckered out from a day of adventure!*

As she slept, Connie dreamt she was accepting an important award for her contribution to science. The judges gave her a crown with "Connie Queen of Slime" engraved on it and everyone wanted to take selfies with her and Big.

Then some special agents in black suits arrived. They wanted to run experiments on her slime. As they carried it away, Big looked at her with the same desperate eyes it had when it fell into the fountain. It reached out to grab her hand.

Connie Queen of Slime! it pleaded.

CONNIE QUEEN OF SLIME! it cried, a little deeper ...

SUNDAY

CHAPTER 13

"CONNIE QUEEN OF SLIME!"

Connie suddenly woke up. Sunbeams crept through a gap in the curtains, bathing Big where it sat on her pillow and giving it an ominous glow.

"GOOD MORNING, CONNIE QUEEN OF SLIME," it announced in a deep voice, so close that Connie could feel its sock-scented breath on her face.

She felt something warm oozing between her fingers. Big was holding her hand with its slimy tendrils. She let go and sat up.

"Apologies, my Queen," Big said, in a voice unrecognisable from the day before. "I should have let you sleep. I was impatient to show you the thorough job I had done in your service."

Her room was spotless.

"What happened?" Connie asked, stunned.

"I tidied your room for you."

"I meant ... your ... the way you're talking ..."

"Oh you're referring to my grasp of linguistics. Yes, it appears I am an amazingly fast learner! I woke up in the middle of the night. Not wanting to disturb you, I busied myself with your collection of educational books and games." Big pointed to the bookshelf. "Don't worry! I returned the fictional pieces in alphabetical order and the non-fiction books in Dewey Decimal order, so you can locate them more quickly. Now, what can I do for you, Connie Queen of Slime? Shall I do your hair? I know all the latest trends from your *Teen Girl Squad* magazine!"

It was a lot to take in first thing in the morning and Connie struggled to respond.

Big was keen to help. "You require sustenance. Shall I fix you some breakfast?"

"Um. No, I can do it. Think I might make

breakfast in bed for Dad."

"Ah. Yes. The father. We mustn't let him know about us."

"Us?"

"I mean ME. We mustn't let him know about me. I have gathered from your historical books that humans attack when faced with things they do not understand. For my safety, I will remain hidden. For now."

In a daze, Connie headed to the kitchen and poured herself a bowl of Crunchy Grain. The smell coming from the jar of Mother no longer bothered her. It smelled better than Big. As she wolfed down her cereal, she debated whether she should be concerned about the rate at which the slime was evolving.

Her thoughts were interrupted by the toast popping up. Connie's dad normally made them soft boiled eggs with soldiers every Sunday, so she cut the slices into narrow strips. As she carried the plate across the living room, she tripped over something. It was the lead from the vacuum she'd left out the night before. She managed to stop herself from falling, but the soldiers weren't so lucky.

"Three-second rule!" she whispered to herself, as she rescued them from the floor and placed them back on the plate.

She gently knocked on her dad's door at the end of the hallway and let herself in.

"What is THIS?" he said in wonder, sitting up in his bed. He clasped his hands in delight as she brought the plate over. "Toast soldiers and ... Oh, just toast soldiers!"

"Uh yeah, I don't know how to do the eggs yet," said Connie, sheepishly. She wondered if Big was already better at cooking than her.

"Well I'm sure your toast is so delicious it doesn't even NEED eggs," he said, taking a bite. He gave a little cough. "... OR butter."

Connie was too distracted to reply.

"But it IS healthier without butter!" he added, not wanting to seem ungrateful.

He coughed again. Bits of bread sprayed from his mouth and showered his duvet. He took a sip of water, but coughed mid-swallow. It shot out his nose like a water slide for bogeys.

"Well, that was undignified," he said, chuckling and wiping his face with his sleeve.

Connie was so busy thinking about Big that she barely noticed. Robotically, she passed her dad a tissue.

"You okay, Con?"

"Yep!" she said, snapping out of it. "Just, lots on today. Allyce's race, Amy's play ..."

"... Your homework, tidying your room ..." he reminded.

"My room's already done!" said Connie. *Thanks*

to Big, she added, in her head.

Her dad was thrilled. "Well then! Sounds like another Pizza Cake night!"

She had to admit, *Baby* Big had been really cute, but *Butler* Big was already proving more useful. Connie decided to stop stressing. She left her dad to finish his toast.

When she opened her bedroom door, she was startled to see Big sitting on her bed, brandishing a large pair of sharp scissors.

"Don't be scared," said Big, sliming over to her. "Snip-snip!"

CHAPTER 14

Connie didn't really want Big to cut her hair, but she'd also seen how quickly Big could turn scary, like how it did with Mike, so she decided it was best to just let the slime do its thing. She sat very still while the sandwich-sized blob oozed over her head with a pair of scissors. It chatted non-stop about art, history and science — everything it had learnt from her books. It was hard to believe that it was the same slime who had barely been able to form a sentence the day before.

After an hour of Big's talkative trimming, Connie started to feel twitchy.

"Is this going to take much longer?" she interrupted. "I don't want to be late for my friends."

"You don't need to see them," said Big, still cutting. "Let's stay here."

Before Connie could argue, the slime did some final flourishes with the scissors and admired its work.

"Are you ready to see your new look, Connie Queen of Slime?"

Connie's stomach churned with a mix of nerves and excitement. Big had taken so long and such care that she'd convinced herself that it was going to be the *best* haircut she'd ever had. She stood up to check the mirror on her wall.

It was *not* the best haircut she'd ever had.

It was the *worst* haircut she'd ever had.

In fact, it was the worst haircut *anyone* had ever had! It was a cross between a bowl-cut and a mullet, with a small fluffy tuft sticking out at the top like a pom-pom.

Her stomach churned again and she vomited a tiny bit into her mouth. She swallowed, trying to ignore the flavour of Crunchy Grains and sick.

The tears were impossible to hold back. It was her own fault for thinking that the super-intelligent sentient slime creature she'd accidentally created was capable of giving her an up-to-date hairstyle, despite it being only two days old.

"What's wrong, my Queen? Don't you like it? I did it exactly like this!" cooed the slime. Big held up her copy of *Teen Girl Squad* magazine and pointed to a model's head.

"THAT'S A HAT!" yelled Connie, between sobs.

She was right. It wasn't a fancy hair-do the model was sporting. It was a fuzzy bobble hat.

"I can't leave the house looking like this!" she cried.

There was a knock at her door. Big dropped the huge scissors and slid under the bed.

"Con? Con! Are you okay? I'm coming in!" called her dad.

He opened the door, took one look at Connie,

and exploded with laughter.

"What did you DO?" he asked through a
fit of giggles. He picked up the discarded magazine.
"It's very impressive. Your hair looks exactly like
this hat!"

"I look hideous!" Connie yelled, pulling the
covers over herself.

"Hey. Don't you go talking like that. You could
shave all your hair off and you would still be the
most beautiful person I've ever seen."

"Well, I guess you haven't seen many people
then!" sobbed Connie, her voice muffled by the
duvet. "Go away. I'm hiding."

"So you're just going to stay in your smelly
room all day?" he asked.

"It's not smelly! YOU'RE smelly!" said Connie,
still hiding under her covers.

Her dad chuckled, "To be fair, it *is* hard to
shower with a bad foot. I probably *am* what smells

seeing as your room is so clean! It looks amazeballs!"

Connie popped her head out from under the covers. "Don't say 'amazeballs', Dad. You're so cringe."

"I'll say whatever you want as long as you keep your room looking like this!"

Connie wiped her eyes with the corner of her sheet.

Her dad sighed, "I can't force you to see your friends, but you still have to do your homework."

"UGH! I hate making posters! And I hate ancient Egypt!" Connie grunted, swinging herself back out of bed.

"That's the spirit!" joked her dad. "AAAHHHH-CHAAAAHHHH!!!" The screezes were back. He excused himself and hopped away, closing the door behind him.

Big slid out from under her bed. Connie shot it a dirty look.

"You did this on purpose so I wouldn't want to go out!" she accused.

Big looked insulted. "I think your hair looks rather fetching! Though, perhaps I could make the bobble more pronounced … snip-snip?"

"Absolutely not."

The slime gave an offended sniff and oozed over to her desk.

"What are you doing?" she asked.

"I'm going to do your homework for you," Big said, pulling out some card from the desk drawer. "A poster about ancient Egypt, did you say?"

"Don't do that," Connie begged.

"Let me win back your trust," pleaded the slime.

"No. I'll do it. Ms Strapp will kill me if I hand in a poster with pyramids that look like hats."

"Who is Ms Strapp?" Big asked, frowning.

"She's my teacher. She's scary. She always takes away my slime and never gives them back."

"There's been *other* slime?" said Big, curiously.

"Not slime like you. Different slime," said Connie. "I didn't make them. They were tubs of slime from the shop. Toys."

"How dull!" snorted Big.

The blob stretched an eerily long, tentacle-like arm across her room and selected a history book from the bookshelf. It was clearly going to make a poster despite Connie asking it not to.

"So I am the only slime like me?"

"I think so," said Connie. "I haven't made any others."

Big seemed slightly disappointed.

Truthfully, Connie didn't know if Big was the *only* living slime out there. It was possible that people all over the world had accidentally made living slime creatures but were hiding them — like she was.

The only giveaway would be their terrible haircuts.

CHAPTER 15

"And the butterfly emerges from its cocoon!" announced Connie's dad from the couch as she entered the living room.

"I need to message Nat. Can I borrow your tablet?"

He pulled a face. "My what?"

Connie sighed. "Can I borrow your *massive phone*?"

"Why, certainly! Just let me finish this call!" He held his tablet to his face. "I HAVE TO GO NOW, YOU TAKE CARE! BYE!" He pretended to hang up.

"Who was it?" asked Connie, playing along.

"Nobel Dad Prize. They wanted to give me the award for being the World's Best Dad," he said, with a grin.

"Again? Wow, that's like, four weekends in a row. Maybe it's rigged?" Connie said, grinning back.

He blew a raspberry and passed her the tablet.

She logged into the chat app.

> Soz, I can't make it today. Can you let Allyce and Amy know?

> NAT
> Why? Are you ok? I told you to see a doctor!

> Don't need a doctor. I made a slime which came to life and cut my hair.

> NAT
> If you're going to lie, at least make it believable.

> I'm not lying! I'll get a better photo of it!

She took the tablet back to her room. Big was busying itself at her desk. She had repeatedly told the slime that she was going to make her own ancient Egypt poster, but Big said it was good to have a back-up, in case she changed her mind.

"Hey Big, I thought it'd be nice to get a photo of us together?"

The slime seemed to like Connie's idea and oozed its way over to her.

"I believe the term is 'selfie'," corrected Big, as it slid up her leg and perched itself on her shoulder. "Make sure you catch my good side."

Connie opened the camera app. She winced at her haircut but was soon distracted by Big making kissing sounds.

"What are you doing?" she asked.

"I read about it in *Teen Girl Squad* magazine. You're supposed to stick your lips out like this." It puckered its mouth.

Connie snapped the selfie. It was a good one. Big's expression was ridiculous, but at least you could see its face. The slime nodded in approval, slid off her shoulder and oozed back to the desk.

With Big distracted, Connie was able to send the selfie to Nat.

> NAT
> **What filter is that?**

> **It's not a filter!**

> NAT
> **It's ok if you're embarrassed that you tried to cut your own hair. You don't have to put a face effect on a slime and make up some crazy story.**

> **Why don't you believe me!**

> NAT
> **You lie a lot. I don't care when it's to other people, but I'm your best friend.**

> **I'm not lying!**

> NAT
> **Whatever. Have fun staying at home with your disgusting blob.**

Nat logged off. Connie felt sick.

Over the years, she had broken a finger, twisted her ankle, and dislocated her elbow. But none of them had hurt as much as losing her best friend's trust.

CHAPTER 16

It was hard for Connie to concentrate on her ancient Egypt poster with her dad's constant yelling. Someone was livestreaming the Community Sports Tournament basketball game so her dad was watching it on his tablet.

"WHAT? WHY WOULD YOU DO THAT?!"

"They can't hear you through the screen, Dad," she said, without looking up. Connie was working at their small dining table because Big had taken over the entire desk in her room.

"UGH!" Her dad made a dramatic point of turning off the livestream and putting down the tablet. "I can't watch this while it's happening. I'll watch the rest later when I know how it ended."

Sounds like Mike's "bad boys" aren't doing too well, thought Connie with a smirk.

The poster was nearly finished – all it needed was a picture. She tried to draw an ibis, but it just looked like an angry duck.

Connie's dad hopped across the living room to see what she'd been working on all afternoon.

"Ooooh!" he said, squinting at her awful handwriting. "Look at all those ... words!"

"This is why we need a printer!" said Connie.

"The ink for those things costs more than the printer itself!" said her dad. "Your handwriting isn't going to get any better unless you practise. It's like your drawing! You used to say you couldn't draw, but look at this ... bird?"

"It's supposed to be an ibis," said Connie.

"Yes, ibis! That's what it's called. It looks exactly like an ibis. Ms Strapp will love it!"

Connie doubted that, but at least she would get a mark for trying.

She went back to her room to see how Big was getting on, but when she opened the door, she couldn't see the slime anywhere.

"You took your time, Connie Queen of Slime," came an ominous voice. "I've been expecting you."

The desk chair slowly swivelled around to face her. Big was sat in it with its blobby arms folded. Connie got the feeling Big was trying to intimidate her, but it wasn't working. The slime was covered in sparkles and had a piece of toilet paper stuck to its head.

"Did you have fun with the glitter?" Connie asked, closing the door behind her so that her dad couldn't hear.

"Yes!" said Big gleefully, before correcting itself. "I utilised the glitter for maximum educational benefit, if that's what you mean. BEHOLD!"

Big moved aside to reveal an incredibly detailed 3D cardboard Egyptian-style pyramid. Connie had to admit, it was very impressive.

"Wow, Big. This is really good! But it was supposed to be a poster," she said, studying it.

"Watch this!"

The slime flicked up a small cardboard latch and the pyramid gracefully unfolded into a four-point-star-shaped glittery poster. Big had written ancient Egyptian facts on each point using strawberry-scented gel pen.

Connie gasped in wonder: it was magnificent. In the centre of the open pyramid was a small cardboard box with hieroglyphs drawn on it.

"What's this bit?" she asked.

"Open it, my Queen!" Big instructed, clasping its blobby hands together in anticipation.

Connie opened the lid of the box. Inside was a small figure bound in toilet paper. A little mummy. She took it out.

"Haha, creepy! This is great, Big! What did you use for the mummy?" As she spoke, it slipped in her hands and the figure unravelled on to the floor. She squealed.

"It's a mouse!" explained Big with pride. "I found it behind the radiator! Don't worry, it is very much deceased. As you can see, it is in quite an advanced state of decay, but I believe the heat must have dehydrated it, helping preserve the body."

It was super gross. Connie made a silent promise to herself to clean more often. She couldn't keep ending up with dead mice in her room.

"Is this the one *you* made?" asked Big, pulling Connie's poster out of her hand and examining it. "Hmm. Not too bad. Why is that duck so angry?"

"It's an ibis!"

The slime studied it closely before putting it down.

"I think you should hand in my poster. It will get you a higher mark," Big said, matter-of-factly.

"It would ..." agreed Connie. "But I worked

really hard on my poster. I don't wanna hand in something I didn't make. It's cheating."

"It's not cheating! You made *me*, so technically anything I *make*, *you* also made!"

It was a good point, but she still felt uncomfortable with the idea.

"I dunno, Big. I still think I should hand in mine," she said, kneeling down and looking around the floor. "Where did that dead mouse go?"

Big mumbled a reply. Connie looked up and noticed the slime's mouth was full.

"Ew! Did you just put it in your mouth? Spit it out! Now!"

"Plegh!" The dead mouse plopped out Big's mouth on to Connie's desk, covered in goo.

"That is DISGUSTING."

Big shrugged, "I was hungry."

"Well, there'll be more tasty hards tonight."

The slime reverted back to its baby state. "Tasty hards?" it said, with big, wide eyes.

Connie's heart softened. "Yeah. No need to eat this!" she said, using the leftover toilet paper to pick up the gooey dead mouse. She carried it towards the door. "I'll just take this away so it's not in my room."

"Be quick," said Big, sounding grown-up again. It lowered its voice to a threatening whisper. "I get lonely when you're not here ..."

CHAPTER 17

Later that evening, as Connie and her dad finished their pizza and watched *Clash of the Cakes: EPIC FAILS*, a rustling sound came from the kitchen.

"I bet it's another ruddy mouse!" he said. "I saw a dead one in the bin, you know!"

Connie knew instantly that the sound wasn't coming from a mouse.

"I'll clean up and go check," she said, picking up the box of uneaten crusts, and heading to the kitchen.

"Okay. Who are you and what did you do with the REAL Connie?" her dad joked, unoriginally.

In the kitchen, Connie found Big rummaging through a cupboard.

"What are you doing?" she whispered, angrily.

"I told you I get lonely, so I am making a friend. I found the formula you used!" Big held up the recipe her dad had written down for her on Friday night.

Connie's dad called from the couch, "Did you say something?"

"Just talking to myself!" Connie called back. She had to get the slime back to her room and fast. She held out a pizza crust and Big dropped the ingredients.

Her dad called again, "What's happening? Is it a mouse?"

"No, all good! No mouse in here! I'm just suddenly tired!" she called, shoving Big and the crusts under her hoodie. As soon as her dad was looking the other way, she made a mad dash for her room.

"Oh! Okay!" her dad called back. "Uh … Goodni—"

Connie slammed her door shut.

CHAPTER 18

Connie was drowning. She tried to swim to the surface, but seaweed kept wrapping around her. First her legs, her arms and then her mouth. She was bound, like a soggy mummy …

She woke up from her nightmare gasping for breath.

It was either really late or really early – the sun wasn't up yet. Big was sitting on her pillow next to her head, watching her in the dark.

"The recipe was wrong," Big growled, glaring at her.

Connie sat up, startled. Big extended its little gooey hands – they were stained green – and dropped a slimy mess on her duvet. It smelled like glue.

"What did you do?" Connie croaked.

"While you were asleep, I followed the slime recipe, but it just made THIS." It gestured to the sticky green gloop. "Make me a friend!"

Connie felt sorry for Big, but she was also beginning to feel scared. "It's the middle of the night," she said. "Later."

"NOW!" demanded Big, through gritted teeth.

Wait— TEETH? Did Big have teeth yesterday? Connie couldn't remember. Either way, she didn't want to see them again.

She groggily got out of bed, scooped up the failed slime from her duvet and tiptoed to the kitchen. Big slid quietly along behind her. She dumped the gluey gunge into a mixing bowl. Then she snuck into her dad's room to get the tub of foot powder from his bathroom.

"AHHHH ... AAHHHH ..."

Connie froze. If her dad

screezed in his sleep, he would definitely wake up. She waited for the inevitable "CHAAAHHH" but instead he let out an extremely loud and incredibly long fart. She slunk out and shut the door before the smell had time to reach her.

Back in the kitchen, Big watched as she spooned the foot powder into the bowl and the mixture became a weird, blue cement.

"I can't wait to go to school with you, Connie," Big said.

Connie wondered whether it was safe to take a slime with teeth to school.

The slime continued, "I need to get smarter to protect you from danger!"

But who will protect me from you? Connie thought.

She emptied a new bottle of liquid soap into the bowl. It was a different brand to the one she had used for Big, but she figured soap was soap. The gunk began to froth. She hesitated. She wasn't ready for another slime like Big — it was hard enough keeping an eye on ONE. She decided not to add the final ingredient.

She took a step back. "Done!"

Big sniffed the bowl.

"No. It doesn't smell right. YOU'RE TRYING TO TRICK ME!" the sludge monster snarled.

Big was on to her. She could see the slime's teeth again. Were they bigger? Sharper? Would it ever hurt her?

She nervously spooned some of the Mother from her dad's jar into the mix. It began to boil and bubble, though this time it didn't turn a yellowy-brown colour, like Big. The new slime was bright pink.

Must be the different brand of soap, thought Connie.

"Smells good!" said Big, ignoring the colour.

"Now put it in the nice warm house so it can incubate." It pointed to the bin.

Connie realised that, as intelligent as the slime had become, there were still a few human things it didn't know. Like what day it was.

Monday.

Bin Day.

"Okay," Connie said, pouring the mixture into the rubbish bin.

"Name it!" ordered Big.

"Uh … Epic Fail," she said, closing the blue lid on the bin.

"Hmm. That's nice," said Big. "What does it mean, Connie Queen of Slime?"

"It's a bit like Big Yikes," said Connie.

CHAPTER 19

Taking Big Yikes to school felt like a bad idea, but Connie had no other choice. It didn't seem safe to leave the slime at home with her injured dad and she didn't want it to notice the rubbish being collected. She also had to prove to Nat that she wasn't lying.

"Have we almost reached our destination?" asked Big, for about the hundredth time.

"Yesss!" chided Connie. "Stop poking your head out!"

Connie was cutting through the park to get to school. It would take longer, but meant fewer people would see the toothy slimeball peeking out from her backpack. It looked like she'd stolen a dog and shaved it.

"Remember, you have to stay in my bag. You

can't let Ms Strapp see you," she reminded Big. If there was one thing she feared more than the slime's new teeth, it was her teacher.

"Ms Strapp doesn't scare me!" Big reassured her.

But it didn't make her feel reassured. If anything, it made her feel more anxious.

Her friends were already at their desks when she got into class. She adjusted the cap she was wearing to cover up her haircut and slid into her chair. Then she spun around to face Nat.

"Do you still think I lied to you?"

Nat looked away, pretending not to hear her.

Connie spotted Mike. "Mike! You've seen my slime! Tell Nat it's real!"

"Dunno what you're talking about, Kenny," he replied.

"Oh really?" shot back Connie. "I brought it

with me, so I'll guess we'll see WHO'S lying at lunch."

The colour drained from Mike's face.

Ms Strapp entered: 9.00 a.m. on the dot.

Connie faced forward again but leaned to one side to whisper to Allyce. "Are *you* peeved at me?"

Allyce shook her head.

Amy leaned over from the other side. "WHAT ARE WE WHISPERING ABOUT?" she said in what could only be described as a "stage whisper".

"Connie wanted to know if we're peeved at her for bailing yesterday," Allyce loudly whispered across Connie's desk.

"Oh!" Amy loudly whispered back. "No. The play was cancelled anyway."

"Why?" whispered Connie.

But before Amy could answer, Ms Strapp placed her hands on Connie's desk and lowered her face to eye-level.

"Can this conversation wait until lunch?" asked their teacher quietly. Ms Strapp's whispering-voice was scarier than her yelling-voice.

Connie gulped and nodded.

"And take that cap off."

Reluctantly, Connie removed the cap. The pom-pom tuft of hair sprang straight up, even though she'd covered it in hair gel. A few kids sniggered. Allyce gasped. Ms Strapp didn't react at all. Connie sank into her chair.

Amy gave a thumbs-up and mouthed, "It looks lit!"

Connie felt a little better until an awful scent wafted across the room. She looked down and noticed the zip on her bag was being edged open from the inside. She hoped Big wasn't trying to burst out so it could defend her.

"What on EARTH is that smell?" asked Ms Strapp, sniffing the air.

The teacher followed the offending odour back to Connie and snatched the bag up off the floor like an eagle swooping on prey. She set the bag on top of Connie's desk and began rifling through it.

"You haven't brought in another slime, have you?" asked Ms Strapp, sternly.

Connie was too afraid to answer. She couldn't think of anything worse than Big squaring up against her teacher. It would be like King Kong versus Godzilla: absolute carnage. Or worse! What if Big and Ms Strapp *teamed up*? She closed her eyes.

"Ah HAH!" said Ms Strapp, pulling something out of the bag. "What do we have here?"

"Ooooh!" said the class, in awe.

Connie opened her eyes. Ms Strapp was holding up Big's ancient Egypt pyramid poster and marvelling at how it unfolded.

The fink! thought Connie. *Big must have*

swapped it out with mine this morning!

Ms Strapp put Connie's bag back on the floor. "Very impressive. But you need to clean your backpack. It smells like dirty socks."

Connie sighed with relief. Unfortunately, the feeling didn't last long.

"I told you mine was better," came a hiss from under her chair.

Sweat started to bead along Connie's forehead. No one else had heard the voice. She felt Big ooze its way up her leg and on to her lap. She looked around nervously to make sure no one else could see.

"I know what's best for you!" it said, through gritted teeth, staring up at her.

Shaking, Connie slowly reached for her bag. She took a deep breath and, with the same skill she used at the checkout to palm tubs of slime, she swept Big into her backpack in one slick move and headed for the door.

"Connie! Where are you going?" barked Ms Strapp.

"I HAVE TO GO TO THE TOILET!" Connie blurted, unable to think of a better excuse.

"Why are you taking your bag?" asked Ryan.

"SOMETIMES GIRLS HAVE TO TAKE THEIR BAGS TO THE TOILET!" Connie replied.

Big let out an audible growl from the bag. Or was it a roar?

"UH-OH! THAT WAS MY STOMACH! BETTER ANSWER NATURE'S CALL BEFORE IT LEAVES A MESSAGE!"

Connie rushed out into the hall. She was dreading the teasing she would get later. But at that moment, teasing was the least of her worries.

CHAPTER 20

Connie burst into the toilets and checked beneath the stalls. Except for one lone shoe (*Seriously, who loses ONE shoe?*), it was empty. She locked herself in a cubicle before opening her bag.

"Why are you ashamed of me, Connie Queen of Slime?" Big asked, angrily.

"I'm not ashamed! I just don't want to get into trouble! I told you before that Ms Strapp hates me bringing slime into school."

"She takes them away and never gives them back," added Big.

"Exactly," said Connie. Big was finally getting it.

"Maybe we should kill Ms Strapp?" Big suggested.

"NO!!!" Connie dropped her bag in shock. As she did, Big fell out of it and landed with a SPLOOSH into the toilet.

Connie's hand trembled. It would be so simple! One push of a button and Big would be gone: flushed out of her life for ever. The slime was becoming too controlling and now it was talking about KILLING her teacher! She may have been terrified of Ms Strapp, but she certainly didn't want to be an accessory to her murder!

Her hand moved towards the flush button, but as she went to press it, Big started splashing around, looking helpless and scared. It reached an arm out towards her, like it had when it fell into the water fountain on Saturday.

She changed her mind and gently scooped the slime out of the loo. Toilet water splashed over her shoes and seeped into her socks. Connie held the slime in her open hands. Big looked up at her with tear-filled eyes and she felt awful for even considering the flush option. It looked like her innocent Baby Big again.

Big stretched out its blobby arms and opened its mouth — Connie assumed to ask for a hug. But instead, it gave a loud COUGH and spluttered up a wet ball of bog roll right on to Connie's top. Big grinned a mischievous smile. Its knife-like teeth were visible again.

"That's better," it growled.

CHAPTER 21

Connie's shoes squelched as she power-walked back to class. Big had reluctantly agreed to stay sealed in her lunchbox until she could introduce it to her friends. She just had to get through the rest of the morning without embarrassing herself any more than she already had.

"Why is there wet toilet paper on your top?" asked Ms Strapp, as Connie entered the classroom.

She had been so busy trying to convince Big not to kill her teacher that she'd forgotten to clean herself up!

JD, who'd been unusually quiet all day, pointed. "What's that in your bag, Connie?"

Before Connie could speak, Ms Strapp fished out the lunchbox. There was a thin layer of yellowy-brown slime on it. The teacher screwed her nose up as the stench wafted back across the room.

Her classmates held their noses. They looked at the toilet paper on Connie's top, then at the yellowy-brown stain on the lunchbox.

"It's not poo!" blurted Connie. "… Just in case you thought it was."

"What is it?" asked JD, concerned.

"It's slime," said Nat, with a glare. "It's all she cares about these days."

"Ah, well you know the rule about bringing slime to school," said Ms Strapp, turning towards the door. "This is going in the Confiscation Cupboard."

"No, you can't! It's a very special slime!" Connie objected.

Ms Strapp frowned. "In that case," she said, "I think I should see this very special slime for myself." She started to open the lunchbox.

"Don't open it!" yelled Connie, terrified that Big would try to attack her teacher. "I can show you a picture! Look …" Connie snatched Nat's phone from her desk. "I sent Nat photos of it!"

"Give me my phone back!" shouted Nat, jumping up. She tried to grab it from Connie's hand, but missed and grabbed Ms Strapp's nose. Everyone gasped.

Ms Strapp snapped. "Right. That's it!" She seized Nat's phone and held it up with the lunchbox. "I'm confiscating BOTH of these!" She strode off towards the staffroom.

Connie sat down, defeated. She could feel the heat of Nat's death stare on the back of her head.

At least Big hadn't attacked anyone.

Yet.

CHAPTER 22

Connie apologised to Nat all through class by whispering and passing notes, but her best friend continued to ignore her. When the bell rang for lunch, Nat marched out without looking at her.

Connie's eyes prickled as she tried to hold back tears. It had been an emotional weekend and a stressful Monday to boot. She wasn't sure she could cope with losing Nat as well.

Amy and Allyce led Connie to an apple tree in a quiet corner of the school yard, which provided a decent amount of shade and privacy.

"Nat's overreacting. She'll get over it," said Amy soothingly.

Connie swallowed the lump in her throat. "She's mad because she thinks I've been lying to her."

"About what?" asked Allyce.

Connie composed herself and took a deep breath. She told Allyce and Amy everything: how she'd been tricking her dad with her 4-Step Slime Heist Plan, how she'd been forced to make her own slime, and how it resulted in a cute little blob called Big Yikes (Big for short) who was alive and could talk, but couldn't swim.

She told them how Big had cut her hair and done her homework, but now it was turning into an uncontrollable monster with sharp teeth. Finally, she told them how she'd tried telling Nat, but because it was so far-fetched, all it had done was make her best friend angry.

By the time she was done explaining, her friends had finished their lunches.

Allyce pulled an apple off the tree and crunched into it. "Okay," she said, through a mouthful. "I believe you."

"You do?" Connie asked, feeling herself

properly relax for the first time in days. "Really?"

"Yeah," Allyce said, still chewing. She shrugged. "Stranger things have happened. Right, Amy?"

Amy nodded. "We can speak to Nat."

Connie shook her head. "She'll just think you're lying and stop talking to you too. The only way I can get her to believe me is to show her Big in the flesh."

Allyce took a big gulp, almost choking on her apple. "You don't mean … ?"

"That's right," Connie said. "I'm going to have to break into the Confiscation Cupboard."

CHAPTER 23

They only had five minutes before lunch was officially over. Thankfully, Connie could see that Ms Strapp and the other teachers were preoccupied with a kerfuffle between some six-year-olds by the playground.

Amy and Allyce stood guard outside the staffroom, just in case any of the teachers returned. Allyce passed Connie her fitness tracker watch.

"I've programmed the alarm to vibrate just before the bell goes, so you have time to get out. Don't mess with any of my apps on there, though, okay?"

"Thanks, Allyce!" Connie said.

She snuck into the deserted staffroom. But something didn't seem right. It smelled different — more musty than usual. Sweaty. Like ...

Dirty socks.

Sure enough, the combination lock on the Confiscation Cupboard was already hanging loose and the door was slightly ajar. Connie's heart sank.

The smell intensified as she pulled the door wide open, revealing a treasure-trove of banned items, including her lunchbox.

"Big!" she said, opening the lid.

But the lunchbox was empty. And there was no sign of Nat's phone.

"Oh no ..." Connie said, under her breath.

"HI MS STRAPP!" she heard Amy and Allyce chirp in unison outside the door.

She was trapped! She jumped into the cupboard and pulled the door shut.

"What are you girls doing hanging around outside the staffroom?" she heard Ms Strapp ask.

"Just grabbing a coffee," she heard Amy respond.

"Very funny, Amy. Now, if I didn't know any better …"

But Ms Strapp was cut off by someone else yelling from down the hallway.

"Shaun's been bitten!"

"Bitten?" repeated Ms Strapp.

Through the crack between the cupboard doors Connie could make out Ms Strapp striding into the room, grabbing a first aid kit and leaving again.

The fitness tracker started vibrating, causing Connie to jump. She grabbed the lunchbox, slipped out of the cupboard and exited the staffroom, just as the end-of-lunch bell rang.

She joined her friends in the hall and held up the empty lunchbox.

"Your slime must have been stolen!" Amy proclaimed.

"It wasn't stolen," said Connie. "It escaped."

CHAPTER 24

They were doing the Beep Test on the outdoor court in PE that afternoon. Everyone had to run between two points every time a beep went off and it got faster and faster. Connie hated it and was out quickly.

Nat was still ignoring her, but Connie didn't have time to worry about that. She kept thinking about Big Yikes's sharp teeth. The slime wasn't in the Confiscation Cupboard, so it must have been running loose in the school.

A nasty thought struck her. *Could Big have bitten Shaun?*

She spotted Shaun by the edge of the court and joined him.

"I heard you got bitten earlier," Connie said.

"I don't want to talk about it," mumbled Shaun.

"What bit you? Was it small? And smelly?"

Shaun slowly nodded.

"Where'd you get bitten?"

Shaun gave Connie a strange look and held up his bandaged hand.

"No, I mean where *were* you?"

"Oh! Near the playground."

"Thanks," said Connie.

She went over to Ms Strapp. "I'm just going to the toilet."

Ms Strapp rolled her eyes and tapped her watch. "Make it quick this time."

The school playground had been vandalised the week before, so the area had been cordoned off by tape, with signs warning children not to play on it. It looked a bit like a crime scene.

When she got closer, Connie sniffed the air. *Dirty socks.*

"Well, well, well ..." came a familiar voice.

She looked up to see Big perched on top of the swing set, picking its teeth with the quill of a feather.

"Big! There you are! I know you bit Shaun!" she said accusingly.

"I did nothing of the sort!"

"Then why are you picking your teeth?"

"Because I just ate a flying tasty hard. Can't say I cared for it. I'm still rather peckish — pun intended." Big laughed and spat out the feather. It floated down and landed by Connie's foot.

"Did ... did you eat a pigeon?" Connie stammered.

"I got hungry. It's tiring work, escaping from a box, inside a locked cupboard, inside a room. Especially while carrying other items." Big held up Nat's phone. "I was going to return your friend's phone and save the day ... But then I had a little look at what was on here …" The slime stared directly into her eyes. It may have been the size of a lunchbox, but it made her feel even smaller. "I know the TRUTH now, Connie! I know how you and your friends regard me! A *disgusting blob*, am I?"

"I didn't say that!" said Connie.

"You didn't exactly deny it! And I found out what 'Big Yikes' and 'Epic Fail' REALLY mean! They're slang terms for MISTAKE! You didn't put me in a 'nice warm house' to incubate, you put me in a bin because you thought I was an accident – nothing but a piece of GARBAGE!"

"You're right," Connie said.

Big blinked, caught off-guard. "I am?"

"Yes. I did think you were a mistake. But that was before I got to know you! Think about all the fun we've had! I even snuck into the staffroom at lunch to find you! I have the empty lunchbox to prove it. Now please, come with me."

Big didn't budge. It was understandably still annoyed. Connie didn't want to be too forceful, not while Big was in such a foul mood. And especially not while it was hungry ... Which gave her an idea.

"Come with me and we can get tasty hards from Pizza Cake after school. Proper, real ones. No feathers."

Big perked up. "You make a very tempting offer, but I don't know if I can trust you any more."

Connie checked the time on Allyce's fitness tracker watch. If she knew where to find Big after school finished, she wouldn't have to worry about keeping it hidden in class. She took off the tracker, tapped it a few times and held it out for Big.

"Fine. You don't have to come with me. Just stay out of trouble and meet me here when this vibrates. I've set an alarm for 3.30 p.m."

"And then fresh tasty hards?" asked Big, taking the watch.

"Yes. Now, can I have Nat's phone back, please?" She reached out her hand.

"No. I think I'll amuse myself with some of the videos available on the YouTubes."

Exasperated, Connie headed back to the court to rejoin her class. She was just in time to see Allyce beating her previous Beep Test record before collapsing in a heap next to her friends amid a round of applause.

"I ... should have ... got my ... fitness ... tracker ... off you ... before ... I did ... that ..." Allyce said between puffs.

"Ah," said Connie. "About your fitness tracker ..."

CHAPTER 25

Back in class, Connie watched the clock intently. Even though she'd found Big, her anxiety was stronger than ever. She couldn't get the image of the chewed feather out of her head.

Allyce hadn't been thrilled about Connie lending her fitness tracker to Big, but she understood that desperate times called for desperate measures. Amy had suggested they all meet Big at the playground after school with Connie. It was a risky move, but it would mean she could finally prove to Nat that she wasn't lying. Then they could ALL go to Pizza Cake together afterwards! She hoped Big would start behaving once it wasn't so hungry.

The bell rang and Connie leapt to her feet, eager to get to Big on time.

"Not so fast," said Ms Strapp, pulling her

aside. She waited until everyone — except Nat — had left and then closed the door. Connie could see Amy and Allyce hovering outside in the hallway.

"Can I check your bag again, please?" asked her teacher.

Connie was grateful to know Big wasn't in it. "Sure!"

Ms Strapp unzipped it and held it upside-down. Dozens of tubs of slime toppled out on to the floor. Nat knelt down and scrambled through them.

"I ... I don't know where those came from," said Connie, genuinely confused.

"Those are from the Confiscation Cupboard," said Ms Strapp. "Now, care to explain how they got into your bag?"

Big!

"It's not here," said Nat, looking up, clearly stressed. Connie glanced at the clock — it was almost 3.30 p.m.

"Did you break into the Confiscation Cupboard and steal Nat's phone, Connie?" Ms Strapp asked.

"No. Well, yes. I mean, I didn't steal Nat's phone," she answered. "But I know who did."

They were interrupted by Amy and Allyce, poking their heads through the door.

"Sorry, Ms Strapp! We just wanted to say we know where Nat's phone is. We think. We were actually going to see if Nat wanted to come with us to get it?"

Ms Strapp sighed. "Fine. You two go reunite Nat with her phone. Connie, sit down please."

"Off to the playground!" yelled Amy, as Nat joined them both.

Ms Strapp pulled up a chair and sat down opposite Connie. "I don't understand this obsession you have with slime. You don't need it. You're so talented."

Connie was expecting a stern telling-off, not a compliment!

"If this is about the pyramid poster, I didn't make it," admitted Connie. "I *did* make one, but it wasn't as good as the one you saw."

Ms Strapp smiled — like an actual smile! It didn't make Connie faint with fear either. It made her feel weirdly warm.

"I wasn't talking about that, but thank you for telling me."

"Oh. I wasn't sure what you meant when you said I'm talented. It's not like I'm good at sport or maths or anything."

"Not all talents are obvious," said Ms Strapp. "Often the least obvious talents are the most useful ones. If you take the time to see them and use them for good, it'll make you happier than any slime ever could."

It turned out that when she wasn't in charge of

twenty-six kids, Ms Strapp was actually quite ... *nice.*

"Did you always want to be a teacher?" asked Connie.

Ms Strapp looked surprised. "Not always. Sometimes I still don't."

Connie was shocked.

"BUT," added Ms Strapp. "I LOVE my job. I wouldn't have it any other way."

The pair sat in a moment of contemplation. It was the first time Connie had seen her teacher as a regular person, not a mean, angry adult. She wondered if she should tell her about Big.

As if reading her mind, Ms Strapp cleared her throat and said, "You know, Connie, if you ever need to talk to an adult about something — especially anything which seems strange or confuses you — you can tell me."

"Well, there is one thing ..." Connie started. But, just as she did, they were interrupted by her three friends at the door.

"It's not there!" Amy said in a panicked tone.

Allyce looked worried. Nat looked furious. Connie checked the clock above the door: it was after 3.30 p.m.

Pizza Cake!

She turned to Ms Strapp. "I'll do detention every day for the rest of this week if you let me go now and get Nat's phone back."

"Where is it?" asked the teacher.

"A friend has it."

"Doesn't sound like a very good friend," said Ms Strapp, raising an eyebrow.

"Maybe not. But Nat is. And I don't want to upset her any more."

Ms Strapp paused while she considered this. "Very well. You can go now. But you have detention *and* litter duty for the rest of the week."

"Thank you, Ms Strapp!" Connie yelled, as she ran out, leaving the pile of old, confiscated slime tubs on the floor.

"And bring in your real ancient Egypt poster tomorrow!" Ms Strapp called after her.

CHAPTER 26

The four friends crossed the main road next to the school and power-walked towards Pizza Cake. Connie tried to explain everything to Nat.

"So if Big isn't at the playground, it might have decided to get tasty hards without me."

"And tasty hards are ...?"

"Pizza crusts," answered Amy and Allyce together.

"I'm not sure if you two should be encouraging this delusion," said Nat, snarkily.

"It's not a delusion!" Connie was getting tired of defending herself to Nat.

"You've had a stressful weekend with your dad's injury, your homework, your haircut ..." said Nat, trying to provide an explanation. "It's very

possible that you subconsciously invented Big Yikes so that everything else seemed less stressful in comparison."

For a brief moment, Connie wondered if Nat could be right. She usually was. But how did it explain the tubs of slime in her bag, or the pyramid poster, or what happened to Mike?

A crash and a scream came from the alleyway behind Pizza Cake.

"Big!" yelled Connie, breaking into a sprint.

In the alleyway, a teenage girl in a Pizza Cake uniform stood in the back doorway, holding a broom like a weapon. Her eyes darted across the bins. A half-eaten rat lay by her feet. It looked like it'd been freshly killed.

"Wha ... wha ..." Connie was too puffed out to talk properly.

126

Allyce caught up with her first. "What's going on?" she said with ease. It was one of the few times Connie felt jealous of Allyce's fitness levels.

"Watch out!" the teenager warned. "There's, like, a feral dog or something out here!"

Connie didn't budge. She knew it wasn't a dog.

Nat and Amy caught up, pausing to catch their breath. "What happened?" they asked.

"Well, we normally get, like rats and stuff out here, because of the leftover food which gets thrown out," explained the teen. "But this thing was different. It had loads of teeth! They were so sharp and scary and ..."

"... Big ..." said Connie, under her breath.

"Yeah, HUGE! Massive pointy ones!" said the teen. "Anyway, it didn't find much, of course. Bins went out this morning. Guess it found this poor little guy though," she said, nodding towards the leftovers of the rat.

A shiver ran down Connie's spine as she imagined Big moving on to larger prey. *Cats ... Dogs ... Babies ...*

As its creator, the slime was her responsibility. If Big ate a bunch of people, then she would go to jail. The thought of disappointing her dad, life behind bars, and having to face the families of those lost to Big's appetite, was terrifying.

"I wouldn't hang around here if I were you," said the teen, gripping the broom as she went back inside.

"We need to stop Big before it starts eating other things," said Connie.

"Hey, look! My phone!" Nat said.

Sure enough, lying amongst the empty bins, was Nat's phone, covered in a thin layer of yellowy-brown slime. Nat picked it up, removed the case and wiped it off with her sleeve.

"Big must have dropped it!" said Allyce.

Nat's bottom lip began to quiver.

"I don't know why you're doing this to me," she said in a quiet voice, tears welling in her eyes.

"Doing what?" asked Amy.

"It was bad enough when my BEST friend" — she looked at Connie — "was lying to me." She turned to Allyce and Amy. "But I don't know why you're both going along with it. Is it some sort of joke? Because it's not very funny. It's just ..." she sniffed, ".. mean "

Connie reached out to hug Nat, but Nat stepped back and hid her face in her hands.

Connie felt awful. She had thought Nat was being a bad best friend for choosing not to believe her, but she'd forgotten that Nat's rational thinking was what she normally loved most about her. It was unfair to expect Nat to react differently. If she wanted her friend's help, she would have to appeal to Nat's logical nature.

"Okay," Connie said. "I know you think Big is just a figment of my imagination. But …
Hypothetically …"

Nat looked up. She liked the word "hypothetical" — they used it in science.

"Hypothetically, if there WAS a sentient slime on the loose, how would you track it down?"

Nat deliberated as she took out a tissue and blew her nose.

"Well, according to you this thing has Allyce's fitness tracker. So if we log on to Allyce's tracker app on my phone, we should be able to see if it's on the move. Or if you're lying and it's just in your pocket."

"Okay," said Connie. "Let's do it."

Nat passed her phone to Allyce so she could log in.

A map of Horror Heights flashed up. They could see a red line showing the route Allyce had

walked to school that day from home. Then it
went a bit squiggly around the school, which must
have been when Connie had passed the tracker to
Big. Then the line went over the main road and
down the alleyway behind Pizza Cake before
backtracking through the school and into the park.
At the end of the line was a flashing dot ... It was
making its way towards Connie's building.

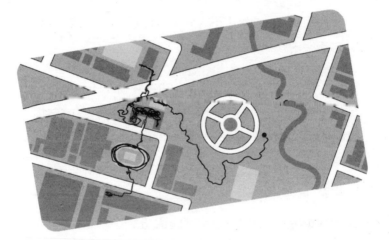

Nat took her phone back and stared at the
map in disbelief. "No way. Some kid must have
stolen Allyce's fitness tracker."

"What?! This is proof I wasn't lying! Give it to me." Connie tried to grab the phone, but Nat fought her off. They tussled.

The phone was still a bit slimy from earlier and was much more slippery without its case. It flew out of their hands like a bar of wet soap and smashed into the ground. The screen looked like someone had tried to hit it with a hammer.

"ARE YOU HAPPY NOW?!" screamed Nat.

"Nat, I'm sorry, just listen—"

"NO! I'm done! I am out! You three can keep playing whatever dumb game this is, but I'M going home!"

Nat picked up her cracked phone and stormed off.

Connie went to follow Nat, but Allyce stopped her. "It was an accident. You've done nothing wrong. Just give her time."

Allyce was right. Connie had bigger concerns. Or, more specifically, BIG concerns. If the slime really was heading back to her place, her dad could be in trouble.

"All right, let's go back via the main road. We might be able to beat it to my flat," said Connie, realigning her priorities. "We have a globby goblin to catch."

"A globlin!" Amy piped up, excitedly.

"Yeah," said Connie, breaking into a jog. "A globlin called Big."

CHAPTER 27

Connie burst through her front door, closely followed by Amy and Allyce. But it was too late.

Her dad lay motionless on the couch with a trail of slime running down his mouth and chest.

"DAD!" Connie screamed. She ran to him, but tripped over the recycling bin.

Her dad sat bolt upright, flinging his laptop across the room.

"GREAT ZOOM MEETING!" he half-yelled, half-snorted, before realising what was happening. "Oh! Connie! Is it the afternoon already? Tell you what, this working-from-home thing is hard!" He looked over her shoulder. "Hi Amy, hi Allyce. Fancy staying for dinner? Is Nat coming?"

"ARE YOU OKAY?! WHAT HAPPENED?" Connie said, scrambling to her feet.

"Well, I managed to bring the bins in, but it was such a pain trying to carry them both with a bad foot that I left the recycling one there," he said, pointing to it. "And then I must have nodded off again."

"BUT WHAT ABOUT THAT?!" yelled Connie, pointing at the slime on his face.

Her dad wiped his chin with the back of his hand. "Oops. Looks like I dribbled!"

Amy and Allyce stifled smirks. Normally, Connie would be embarrassed, but this time she was relieved.

Her dad grabbed a *Clash of the Cakes* magazine. "I'll just have a quick bath to wake up and then maybe you three can help me with the sourdough. We'll have freshly baked bread with dinner!" he said, hobbling down the hall to the main bathroom. "Oh and Con, could you put away the recycling bin and the vacuum cleaner please? This is starting to look less like a living room and more like an obstacle course!"

Tidying could wait. Connie retrieved her dad's laptop from the floor. Fortunately, it had survived much bigger incidents, like the time she spilt lemonade on the keyboard and the "O" key stopped working. Until it was fixed, Connie had to make sure any projects she typed up didn't have the letter "O" in them. Which was why she once had to write an essay about the ozone layer called, "*Earth's Special Bubble Thing*".

"Allyce, can you log on to your fitness tracker account on the laptop?" she asked.

"You bet!"

The map loaded and, sure enough, the flashing dot was out the other side of the park and making its way to Connie's place.

"It's coming," Connie said, anxiously. "It'll be here any minute."

Amy grabbed an umbrella which was hanging

up by the front door. Connie and Allyce looked at her.

"What?" Amy said. "We're about to meet a globlin capable of biting the head off a live rat I want to be armed!"

It actually made a lot of sense. Connie picked up a chair. Allyce chose a basketball.

"A basketball? What are you gonna do with that? Challenge it to a three-point shootout?" teased Connie.

"I could basketball it in the face! No one likes getting basketballed in the face!" said Allyce.

Just then, there was a frenzied knocking at the door, followed by several rings of the doorbell. The three of them froze.

"Connie ..." said Amy. "Can globlins ring doorbells?"

Connie held a finger in front of her lips, motioning for them to be quiet. She snuck up to the front door. Amy lifted the umbrella ready to strike, while Allyce grasped the basketball tightly. Connie raised the chair with one hand, like a lion tamer, and turned the doorknob with the other. In one stealthy move, she flung the door open.

"IT'S REAL AND IT'S COMING THIS WAY!" yelled Nat, tumbling into the flat.

Nat straightened herself up and caught her breath. She looked around at them all. "Why are you holding a chair?" she asked Connie, before noticing Allyce. "Were you going to basketball me in the face?"

"Uh … no …" Allyce tried to hide the ball behind her back, but instead ended up throwing it into the coffee table with a crash.

"IS EVERYTHING OKAY OUT THERE? IS THAT THE GROCERY DELIVERY?" called Connie's dad from the bathroom.

"NO, IT'S NAT, DON'T WORRY!" yelled Connie.

"OH HI NAT! ARE YOU STAYING FOR DINNER, TOO?"

"UH, SURE!" Nat shouted in a panic. She turned back to Connie. "I'm so sorry, Con. I should have believed you! I just ... it's just so ... it makes no sense ... but its TEETH, Connie, its TEETH!" She began to hyperventilate.

"It's okay, Nat! Just breathe. In ... and out ... in ... and out ..." Connie took Nat's hand and led her to the sofa to sit down. "Tell us what happened."

After a few deep breaths, Nat started again. "I decided to walk home through the park and I saw it."

"The slime?" asked Connie.

Nat nodded. "It was heading this way, darting from bush to bush, leaving a sticky, gooey trail. At first I thought it was my imagination. But then I heard it speaking to itself. It kept saying, 'Connie Queen of Slime' over and over again. And that's when I knew it was real and it was coming for you. I ran here as quickly as I could!" She started sobbing. "I'm so sorry!"

Connie hugged Nat. "No, I'M sorry! I got your phone confiscated and then broke it!" she cried.

The moment was ruined by a wet clapping sound.

Connie lowered her voice. "Did anyone shut the front door?".

"HOW VERY TOUCHING," came a growl from the entrance. Big was slapping its blobby arms together in a slimy attempt at an evil slow clap. Allyce's fitness tracker sat on its head like a crown.

"Big! There you are!" said Connie, jumping to her feet. "I've been looking all over for you! I was going to take you to Pizza Cake! Mmm, tasty hards! Remember?"

"Don't patronise me," sneered Big. "I waited for you and you never came."

"I did! I was just late because I had detention!"

"DON'T INTERRUPT ME," roared Big. It was small, but had the voice of a giant. "I went to Pizza Cake WITHOUT you. All I found — besides a loathsome, furry excuse for a tasty hard — were some EMPTY bins. That's right! APPARENTLY the rubbish was collected today … So much for my new companion! It was the ONE thing I EVER asked you for!"

"Oh dear, what a shame," Connie said, pretending she didn't know it was Bin Day. "I'll make you a new one, Big!"

"DON'T CALL ME THAT," it bellowed. "You LIED to me, Connie. You lied about what I am! You lied about creating a friend for me! You lied about getting me tasty hards! And that makes me angry and lonely and hungry! So now, if you'll excuse me, I need to get to work." Big slid past and into the kitchen.

"Are you making a sandwich?" Connie asked hopefully.

"No," said Big. "I'm going to make an army — and this time, I'LL name them. Then, while I wait for them to incubate, I'm going to eat you and your friends and everyone you love. YOU will be the tasty hards!"

"Hah! You don't scare us!" said Amy. "You're tiny!"

"Oh, am I?" said Big. It slowly opened its mouth as it slithered towards them. Its lower jaw remained on the floor, but its upper jaw extended eerily high, past their heads. New teeth started to appear around the edges, until Big was just a giant mouth. It could probably swallow all four of them without chewing.

The friends froze — except for Amy. She bravely lunged at Big and stabbed the umbrella right into its gaping jaw. Then she did something a superstitious person would never do: she opened it inside.

It sprang out with a WHOOSH and stretched Big's gob like a frisbee in a balloon.

"AHHHHHHHH!" howled Big. But it wasn't a howl of pain, it was a howl of laughter! "HAHAHAHAHAHAHAHA!"

Big crunched its mouth shut and the umbrella snapped like a twig. "Isn't it bad luck to open an umbrella indoors?" the slime chuckled, completely unscathed.

"WHAT ARE YOU LOT UP TO OUT THERE?" called Connie's dad from the bathroom

Big licked its lips and headed towards the hallway. "Mmm. Perhaps there's time for a father-shaped snack before I get to work on my army ..."

"BASKETBALL IN THE FACE!" yelled Allyce, as she picked up the basketball and threw it as hard as she could at the beast. The creature recoiled – not even Big was immune to being basketballed in the face.

"RUN!" shouted Connie, grabbing her friends and making a dash for the hallway.

They slammed the door and leaned up against it, shutting Big on the other side.

"I HEAR BANGING!" called Connie's dad, sternly.

"WE'RE, UH ... PLAYING BASKETBALL!" Connie called back through the bathroom door.

"FINALLY! TRY NOT TO BREAK ANYTHING AND I'LL TEACH YOU KIDS SOME TRICK SHOTS LATER! – AHHHH-CHHAAAAAHHH!"

Nat pointed at their feet. "Uh, Connie! We have a situation!"

A small pool of goo was seeping into the hallway from under the living room door. As they watched in horrified fascination, Big's mouth slowly formed on the floor.

"Good idea," said the mouth. "You stay here, out of the way, while I make the army. THEN I'll eat you all." The mouth slid back under the door and disappeared.

The four friends exchanged worried looks. They'd gone in search of Big without a plan for how to stop it. Now they were trapped and about to die.

Worst. Monday. Ever.

Connie felt terrible. If she hadn't involved her friends, they'd be safe. The only thing worse than being eaten alive by a sentient slime with multiple rows of dagger-like teeth was knowing that, because of her, her friends and father were also going to be eaten alive by a sentient slime with multiple rows of dagger-like teeth.

"Maybe we should call the police?" suggested Allyce.

"To do what? Arrest it? How would they even put the handcuffs on?" said Nat.

Amy was still optimistic. "We just need a plan!"

A plan.

Connie tried to focus, but all she could hear was her heart beating and the sound of her dad happily splashing about in the bath.

Hang on. Water …

Suddenly, everything became clear.

Connie motioned for them to form a huddle and she lowered her voice to a whisper. "I've got a plan! A 4-Step Plan, in fact!" She grinned. "We are about to pull off the biggest slime heist of our lives …"

THE
4-STEP
SLIME HEIST
PLAN

MONSTER
EDITION

CHAPTER 28

STEP 1: The Helpful Assistant

The first thing they needed to do was buy some time. Nat strode into the kitchen, which took Big by surprise. The slime was still tall, but had reduced the size of its mouth, much to Nat's relief.

"Thought you might need this," she said, popping several large tubs of foot powder on the counter.

"I *do* actually ..." snarled Big. It ran a slimy tongue across its teeth. "Why would you try to help me?"

"I had another fight with Connie. I said she was wrong to underestimate you. You're obviously highly intelligent. I know what it's like to feel left out for being clever. I'm Connie's smartest friend — well, I WAS Connie's smartest friend. We're not friends any more. I need to start hanging out with more intellectual beings. Like you."

Big relented. "Fine! You can help me make the army. I'm still going to eat you afterwards, though."

"I've accepted that," said Nat. She lifted up the blue lid on the empty rubbish bin. "Hey, if you use this instead of a bowl, you could make a bigger army!"

"Yes. Good idea ..."

While Nat was in the kitchen with Big, Connie was in her dad's bedroom with Allyce and Amy.

"Why did Nat give Big the foot powder?!" asked Amy. "Now the globlin will be able to make its army!"

"Stopping the army won't stop Big," said Connie. Then she held up a drink bottle. "But this will."

"Is water really the best weapon?" asked Allyce.

Connie gave a sly smile. "It is if you can't swim."

STEP 2: The Sprint

While Nat kept Big busy in the kitchen, Allyce sprinted to the living room and quietly poured water into the empty recycling bin. Then she ran back to the en suite to refill it again. And again. And again. Allyce's experience with the Beep Test was paying off. Within five minutes, she'd almost filled the bin up to the top.

"It's a shame this isn't an Olympic event," said Connie.

Amy loudly whispered in a fake announcer voice, "And, representing Horror Heights in the Water Bottle Relay, it's Allyce!"

Allyce returned with the empty bottle. "Okay, the bin's full. I put the yellow lid on so Big won't see what's in it."

"Good," said Connie. "Amy, you'll need to use your acting skills to create a diversion."

"Not a problem," said Amy. She clicked her

fingers. "You said Big was the one who gave you that ridiculous haircut, yeah?"

"Hey! You said it looked lit!"

Amy looked smug. "I'm a VERY good actor, Connie."

STEP 3: The Misdirect

Back in the kitchen, Nat and Big were using the empty rubbish bin to make a massive batch of slime. They poured multiple bottles of liquid soap into the mix and the gloopy, foot-powdery mess changed colour and thickness. All that was left to do was add the Mother.

They looked up as Amy sauntered in with a coy expression on her face.

"What do YOU want?" grunted Big suspiciously. "To be an appetiser?" One of its teeth glinted under the kitchen's fluorescent light.

"Well, firstly, I wanted to apologise for stabbing you in the mouth with an umbrella. It was rude of me. I'm sorry I hurt you."

"You didn't hurt me," Big grunted again. "I can't be hurt."

"Right! Right, of course. Anyway, I was thinking ... Seeing as you're going to eat us soon, I'd like to at least look really good when I die." Amy traced her toe across the floor. Big ignored her, so she continued. "I'd LOVE a haircut as cool as Connie's."

Big chuckled. "I'm not falling for that. You're trying to distract me."

"I knew it!" exclaimed Amy.

"Knew what?" Big asked.

"I KNEW Connie was lying to me! She said YOU cut her hair, but I said that was impossible because it was too professionally done. It must have been cut by someone who had been training for YEARS."

Big scowled. "I DID cut Connie's hair!"

"It's okay, you don't have to lie to me. Not everyone can cut hair," said Amy, reeling Big in.

Big pulled some scissors out of the kitchen drawer. "YOU, KEEP MIXING," it barked at Nat. Then it turned back to Amy. "ALL RIGHT. YOU. SIT."

Amy perched on the counter so that Big had to turn its back to the doorway. She was suddenly aware that she was going to have to stay perfectly still, while the slime wielded a pair of scissors dangerously close to her face. Out the corner of her eye, she saw Connie crawling into the kitchen.

STEP 4: The Switch

Big ran its slimy fingers — if you could call them that — through Amy's hair. She closed her eyes and tried not to seem disgusted.

"Hmm ..." it muttered. "I think I'll give you the same cut I gave Connie."

"Ohh ... goodie ..." said Amy, in feigned excitement.

"So, where are you going for your holidays?" asked Big. "Just kidding, I know where you're going! My belly!" The globlin chortled and slapped its stomach.

Amy nervously laughed along. She opened one eye to see a slimy blade hovering in front of her face, positioned to cut quite a large chunk of hair off. She winced and waited for the SNIP; but instead, all she heard was the hollow sound of something plastic hitting the floor and rolling away.

Amy opened her other eye to see that Connie had knocked over one of the empty liquid soap bottles as she left the kitchen.

Unfortunately, Big saw it too.

The slime dropped the scissors and spun around. Its mouth extended again, in a twisted scowl of teeth and dripping saliva. It moved with ferocious pace towards Connie, who was trying to hide the bin outside the kitchen door. Its eyes burnt with fury.

"YOU THINK YOU CAN SABOTAGE MY PLAN WITH A SIMPLE SWITCH TRICK?!" Spit flecked out as Big gave a deep laugh. "YOU THINK I WOULDN'T NOTICE YOU SWAPPING THE BINS AND TAKING AWAY THE ONE I'M MAKING MY ARMY IN?" It pointed to the lid on the bin back in the kitchen. "YOU THINK I'M SO STUPID THAT I WOULDN'T KNOW THAT THE YELLOW LID IS THE RECYCLING BIN?" Then it pointed to the lid on the bin Connie was trying to obscure. "AND THE BLUE LID IS THE RUBBISH BIN?"

"Uh-oh, you got me!" said Connie.

Big shoved her to the side and lifted the blue lid, expecting to see the slime mix.

"WHAT IS THIS? WHERE IS MY ARMY?!"

"NOW!" shouted Connie.

CHAPTER 29

Nat and Amy ran at Big from behind, while Connie and Allyce came in from the sides. They knocked the slime monster over so that it toppled into the bin full of water, head-first. Big reeled in shock, shrinking back down to the size of a lunchbox again.

Connie leaned over it. "I didn't switch the *bins*, Big. I switched the *lids*. We outsmarted you."

Big thrashed about. It coughed and spluttered and choked. It was defeated ... They thought.

The thrashing turned into a familiar rhythm. Connie gasped. Big was doing backstroke.

"Oh yes, I should have thanked you, Nat, for lending me your phone," it said, looking up at them, mid-stroke. "It's amazing what you can learn from internet videos, isn't it? All sorts of skills ... like swimming."

It winked at them and did a flawless underwater somersault. Then it opened its jaw so all the water gushed into it, like a whirlpool. Its mouth became the width and depth of the bin. Big looked like a garbage bag crossed with a shark.

With one GULP the water was gone and Big started to grow again. The bin strained at the sides – stretching until it couldn't take any more – and exploded. Big expanded to the height of the ceiling. It peered down at them and, with a deafening boom, said:

"More like

MASSIVE Yikes,
am I right?"

The girls tried to back away as it loomed.

"What, you don't think that's funny? That's fine. I don't need you!" Big thundered. **"ALL I HAVE TO DO IS ADD THE FINAL INGREDIENT! I'LL FINISH THIS ARMY ON MY OWN AND DEVOUR EACH AND EVERY ONE OF YOU."** It stared at Connie.

"I'LL START WITH YOUR FATHER. THEN YOUR FRIENDS. THEN I'M GOING TO EAT YOU, SLOWLY, FROM YOUR TOES UP SO THAT YOU HAVE TO WITNESS ALL OF IT."

The friends cowered as it towered over them. They had tried everything, but Big was impervious to their attacks.

"If only this was DaVerse," whimpered Nat.

Something clicked in Connie's mind. She looked around the room and spotted it.

She dived, grabbing the vacuum cleaner.

"Hah!" laughed Big. **"You think you can suck me up? Your vacuum doesn't scare me!"**

"Yeah?" said Connie, with a wry smile. "Well, it should!"

Connie slammed the "reverse" button, took aim, and released a spray of dust into the slime's jaws.

Big gulped, blinked and then instantly started shrinking.

"NOOOOooooooooooo!!!!"
screeched Big.

The creature shrivelled up, its voice getting higher and higher as it got smaller and smaller.

"After everything I did for yooouuuuuuu!"
it squealed, until its mouth was too tiny to be heard and its eyes glazed over, frozen for evermore.

"THAT WAS AMAZING!" yelled Nat.

"Couldn't have done it without you," said Connie.

"Uh … what just happened?" asked Allyce.

"Dust," explained Connie. "Slime's worst enemy!"

CHAPTER 30

Connie stared at what was left of Big: a tiny, hard plastic nub the size of her palm. She wondered if it could still see her out of its unblinking eyes. She wasn't scared any more, but its stone-like expression gave her the creeps, so she wrapped it in toilet paper, like a little mummy.

It's what Big would have wanted, she thought, as she covered up its withered face and popped it in her pocket.

The door burst open, causing all four to jump.

"WHAT HAPPENED IN HERE?!" yelled Connie's dad. He was dressed (thankfully) and had his hair up in a towel.

Connie paused. She wanted to tell her dad the truth — but she knew there was no way he would believe her.

Nat spoke for her. "We made a mess, so I tried to clean it up, but accidentally had the vacuum on reverse!" she said, slapping her forehead.

Connie's dad eyed them all, but before he could ask any questions, the doorbell rang. They exchanged nervous glances as he limped over to answer it.

"Dad, be care—"

"GROCERIES!" he cheered, opening the door to reveal the delivery driver. "Just in time — we've been getting through a heck of a lot of liquid soap lately!"

CHAPTER 31

The friends re-vacuumed up the dust and emptied it into the real rubbish bin to soak up the unfinished mixture. They couldn't risk a potential slime army getting made!

As they helped unload the shopping bags in the kitchen, Connie's dad pulled her into the living room.

He held out a tub of slime.

"I added it to the online grocery order," he said with a wink. "To thank you for being so helpful while my foot heals."

Connie's gut wrenched. She knew she had to come clean. After all, it was her lies which had made it so difficult for others to trust her.

"Dad, I have to tell you something," she said. Her mouth felt dry. She spoke quickly, without taking a breath, "I've-been-sneaking-tubs-of-slime-into-the-shopping-without-you-knowing!" It was like ripping off a band-aid.

"Oh Con," said her dad, sounding disappointed. "I knew that!"

"Wait, what?"

"Yeeeah," he said, sheepishly. "I was going to say something sooner, but I was trying to work out how you were doing it! It was like watching a magician! There were some weeks when I was sure you hadn't managed it, but then I'd check the receipt and somehow there'd be a new slime on there!"

"Why didn't you say anything when I lied to you about needing one for school?" Connie asked, feeling ashamed.

Her dad shrugged, "I wanted to see if slime meant so much to you that were willing to make your own."

"Well, I'm over slime now," she said. "I'll pay you back and I promise to never trick you again. Unless you know it's a trick."

"Oooh yes! I want a ticket to see The Amazing Connie-ni!"

"Thanks, Dad. I love you."

"I love you too, Con," he said, giving her a hug. "Guess I'll keep this tub for myself then." He hobbled off towards his room. "Just call me *Daddy Queen of Slime*!"

CHAPTER 32

Back in the kitchen, the others were reliving the afternoon's excitement. When Connie returned, Amy was doing an impression of Big while Allyce and Nat pretended to shoot her with the vacuum cleaner. They cheered as she joined them and for a moment, Connie saw herself through their eyes. They were proud of her, and she was proud of herself too.

Ms Strapp had been right about less-obvious talents being more useful: her ability to improvise had saved their lives.

Nat put her arm around Connie. "Next time you make a smelly, evil, colour-changing slime with teeth, I'll believe you!"

"There WON'T be a next time. Trust me!" Connie laughed. Then she stopped. "Wait, what do you mean *colour-changing*?"

"You know! How Big changed colour before it got here!"

Connie was puzzled. "Big didn't change colour. Big was yellowy-brown from the start — ever since I added the Mother."

"That can't be right!" Nat said.

"Why not?"

"Because the slime *I* saw in the park wasn't yellowy-brown!"

Connie's expression turned from confusion to dread. "… What colour was it?"

"… Bright pink."